LET ALL OUR GHOSTS DEPART

Advance Praise for *Let All Our Ghosts Depart*

"Meghana Mysore's language feels lived-in and is beautifully concerned with 'the constant little tragedies of living,' especially those tragedies tied to families, distance, sublimated trauma, storytelling, and death of a loved one. In melancholic and poetic prose that reflects the characters' psychic distance from the worlds they inhabit, the stories in *Let All Our Ghosts Depart* explore powerful themes through the eyes of women longing to find connection and meaning across several generations of dislocation."

—Jessie Ren Marshall, award-winning playwright and author of *Women! In! Peril!*

"*Let All Our Ghosts Depart* is a work of wonder. Kaleidoscopic and introspective, this book is a testament to the expansive and transformative power of storytelling. Examining grief and loss, loneliness and intimacy, the longings and desires of women, and the tarnished brightness of being alive, these stories are as multifaceted as memory itself. They are deeply wise, layered, and full of light. Carefully and lovingly observed, with great empathy for its characters and their endless depths, these stories illuminate the lives of mothers and daughters, grandfathers and siblings, ghosts and the living, lineage and futurity, memory and possibility. With both essayistic precision and poetic mystery, this book illuminates the selves we once were and are always in the process of becoming.

—K-Ming Chang, Lambda Literary Award–winning author of *Bestiary*, *Gods of Want*, and *Organ Meats*

"*Let All Our Ghosts Depart* is an extraordinary collection in its inventiveness and originality, and in its creation of distinct and unique characters. Meghana Mysore's glorious debut explores experiences of the Indian American diaspora with beauty and precision and humor; she writes about grief and longing like no one else. A magnificent collection."

—Karen E. Bender, author of *The Words of Dr. L and Other Stories* and *Like Normal People* and National Book Award Finalist

"In these visionary stories ex-lovers metamorphose into strangling scarves and three generations of women joyfully transform into rainbow-hued squirrels; the dead refuse their deaths even as the living must fight to be alive. Every page offers something gorgeous, savage, and unexpected. Meghana Mysore is an extraordinary talent, and her work is unforgettable."

—Susan Choi, National Book Award–winning author of *Flashlight* and *Trust Exercise*

"There's a strangeness born of real life that only fiction can reach; these haunting, wholly original stories illuminate the ways in which we both connect with and miss the most important people in our lives."

—Sejal Shah, author of *How To Make Your Mother Cry: Fictions* and the essay collection *This Is One Way to Dance*

"*Let All Our Ghosts Depart* is a beautiful and imaginative collection, filled with characters who are longing to make sense of themselves, their relationships, and the losses that haunt them. With humor and insight, these stories ask us to reflect on what we owe each other and ourselves. A thrilling debut."

—Marian Crotty, author of *Near Strangers* and *What Counts as Love*

LET ALL OUR GHOSTS DEPART

STORIES

MEGHANA MYSORE

WEST VIRGINIA UNIVERSITY PRESS | MORGANTOWN

Epigraph from Lucille Clifton, "won't you celebrate with me" from *The Book of Light*.
First edition published 2026 by West Virginia University Press
Printed in the United States of America
ISBN 978-1-959000-94-5 (paperback) ISBN 978-1-959000-98-3 (epub)
ISBN 978-1-959000-99-0 (PDF)

Library of Congress Cataloging Number: 2026013707

Cover design by Elisha Zepeda
Book design by Kelley Galbreath
Cover image courtesy of Meghana Mysore
Author Photo by ©2025 Michael Verity Photography. All Rights Reserved.

For EU safety/GPSR concerns, please direct inquiries to WVUPress@mail.wvu.edu or our physical mailing address at West Virginia University Press / PO Box 6295 / West Virginia University / Morgantown

For my family, in the blue house
near the end of the street.

WON'T YOU CELEBRATE WITH ME

won't you celebrate with me
what i have shaped into
a kind of life? i had no model.
born in babylon
both nonwhite and woman
what did i see to be except myself?
i made it up
here on this bridge between
starshine and clay,
my one hand holding tight
my other hand; come celebrate
with me that everyday
something has tried to kill me
and has failed.

—*Lucille Clifton*

CONTENTS

LET ALL OUR GHOSTS DEPART

HOARDER

AT MY APARTMENT COMPLEX'S scarf sale, I tried to give away my last boyfriend. But E was such a beautiful and soft red scarf. He smelled like pumpkin spice. A pumpkin-spice-smelling scarf is too unique to give away. I didn't want some other person enjoying the spices of my labor. So I wrapped him around my shoulders and left.

In my apartment, I put him back on the table with the Trader Joe's succulent that I was slowly letting die. I knew how to let go—but only to a succulent that I didn't think was very pretty (just very prickly).

I went over to my French press to make myself an afternoon cup of coffee. I had been trying to cut down on my coffee intake, but, you know, we all have our vices. I'd left N near the sink. I pulled them away. I didn't want their rich emerald-green silk to be damaged by a sudden spurt of water. This sink was unpredictable. I had to put in a maintenance request. I patted them, feeling their smoothness.

N was always very nice to me; they would bring jars of almond butter to our dates because it was the only nut butter I wasn't allergic to. I liked their facial hair, liked its roughness on my face. On Sundays, they would cook me meals of spaghetti and soup, and we'd watch old episodes of *Scrubs*. They moved back to Texas at the end of our summer romance because their mother was dying. They posted a picture of the quilt she turned into on Facebook. It had many blue dots on it. I "love"-reacted to the picture. I fell asleep on the couch with scarf-them often. When we broke up and they turned into a scarf, we were sitting together on a bench in the park we went to on Sundays. A little girl ran in front of us and stuck out her tongue. I stuck my tongue out back at her but then realized that it wasn't cute when grown women did this, only kids.

Today was a Saturday, and when I wasn't writing an instruction manual for work, I was listening to the Maisy Poppens podcast. I had started listening a few months ago when an episode called "Scarf Hoarders: Three Research-Backed Habits That Will Allow You to Let Go" appeared on my Instagram. I clicked on it mostly because her last name was Poppens. I hoped that she, like Mary Poppins, would be an efficient lady with magical powers to fix my life; I could see her using an umbrella as a parachute.

I had been listening to Maisy Poppens so much that I barely had any free time to socialize with other human beings. Her voice drowned out the noise in my head. Mostly, the noise was my friend Mira's voice. I stopped talking to her when I graduated from college, after my sister died. Mira was my best friend in college. We used to go for night runs that quickly turned to night walks where we got ice cream at the end. I remember the sticky blue ice cream on my hands, and Mira wiping it away with a napkin. I remember how she took care of me in these small ways and how much I needed this tenderness.

I closed the blinds to prepare for listening to a Maisy Poppens episode. I wanted to be in my little self-help podcast cave with my scarves and my quilts.

The general recommendation was that people kept only four quilts throughout their lifetime of those who had passed on, and five scarves from breakups. Every apartment complex or neighborhood community held monthly scarf sales. I was only halfway there on the quilt recommendation. My sister and my grandmother. As for the scarves . . . my whole room was filled with them—under my pillows, on the floor. In the kitchen. On the tables. I had had lots of short relationships, some medium-length ones, and lots of people who had left me. And I couldn't let go of them, though I tried. In the winter, their wool kept me warm.

It was always strange when a lover broke up with you and transformed into a scarf. I thought it would become less strange with each transformation, but no. I thought back to a few of them. With S, I was on top of him when he declared, "I'm just not feeling this anymore." And then I was above a radiant purple scarf. With B, we were biking together when he fell into a bush and then wordlessly became a green stretch of fabric running along the leaves.

Every time, I was left with a new scarf but not just that. In the past few years, I had also developed swirls of color on my leg. The swirls started blooming on me when my sister was dying. When I felt something I could not name, my legs were littered with these abstract stains, each of them alive with feeling. When I pressed on them, I felt the ache, and it led me back to a memory.

Not everyone was stained with emotion in this way. But many women in my family were. My sister and my grandmother most strongly. It was what had killed them. I had seen Ajji's left leg when I was a child. I saw her wrap herself in a towel after a shower. I had gasped because my legs were unstained then. I stared at my own blank, brown legs and then at hers, neon purple and green skating on her skin. I gasped and wished that I would not also inherit this disease of incessant feeling.

In recent years, it was always after seeing my legs in their neon glow that my lovers left me. It could take a month, or even half a year, after the moment of seeing, but it became a predictable trajectory. We'd be talking about a passage of a book, or holding one another on the couch, and I'd think it was safe to show them. I would feel a warm tickling in my thighs as emotions blossomed on my skin, and I'd lift up my dress or skirt so they could share in this part of me. I watched their faces as their lips moved and eyebrows scrunched, and I waited for their words. They touched each spot of color, and I would feel the awakening of desire, and I'd whisper, "Soft, soft." So before they left me, they ran their palms softly over the rivers of color, telling me stories about beauty and the canvas of me.

Mira was different. We never called each other lovers, and we never so much as kissed, but when she saw my legs, she felt them and didn't run away. I showed her the swirls when they first started appearing. We were on her bed, in her dorm room, reading Anne Carson's "The Glass Essay." Mira was obsessed with this poem, with the images of the Nudes. When we finished reading the poem this time, I didn't say anything, just stared out ahead.

She asked me what I was thinking about, and I told her.

My sister, in the hospital bed, eating applesauce. It was all she could stomach in the last month of her life. My mom sleeping next to her, hand resting on her belly, where the hurt lived. My mother's belly, where my sister once lived.

When we were little, my sister and I used to play games of pretending. At the beach, we pretended we were the silent stones. We pretended we were seaweed. We pretended we were the clouds in the sky.

My sister had inherited the disease of incessant feeling, and it engulfed her. She had rainbow swirls not only on her legs but on her belly, and the doctors found solid masses of rainbow in her stomach. "Like tasty little lollipops!" one had remarked, trying to make her laugh, but she just stared back at him blankly.

I'd seen her standing naked in front of the full-length mirror in her room before a doctor's appointment. She was fourteen then; not long after, she died. She looked like a painting, coils of yellow and slivers of rainbow dancing on her body. I watched her as she touched every place of color. The trouble was that her body couldn't hold all the feelings. For one moment, I saw her look at herself as if all the trouble had shivered out of her. She smiled.

After recounting this, I guided Mira's hand to the fabric of my jumper and pulled up the pant legs. "It's starting to happen to me," I said. "I noticed it yesterday."

She touched my skin, circling the spots with her finger, as if they were something to love.

By the following weekend, I was getting a little tired of my self-help podcast cave. It was when I was lying on the ground, under a sea of ex-lover scarves while simultaneously eating handfuls of Flamin' Hot Cheetos, that I decided something needed to change. With my red-Cheeto-dust-covered hand, I reached for my phone to pause the podcast episode that was playing. Also, Maisy's voice was starting to piss me off. I had an idea. Maybe I had to make more direct contact. I would email Maisy Poppens, and I'd ask her what to do.

I felt determined, so I wrote the email quickly.

> *Hi, my name is Alia. My sister passed away five years ago, and I can't bear to look at the quilt-her still. Since then I've been in a series of relationships that all ended and I can't give away the scarves of these past lovers. I fall asleep under them almost every night. I've cut out most living people from my life and just listen to you over and over again. Most people run away from me when they see what's inside. I want to feel connected to the world again. I don't know how. Can you help me?*

I didn't expect a response. Her inbox must have been filled with thousands of pleading emails like mine. But she wrote back to me the next day.

> *Dear Alia, Thank you for your email. Your message has inspired me to make an episode on moving through grief and connecting with others. I would like to invite you to take part in a one-on-one live coaching session with me next Friday. I think your story would be very powerful for our listeners. You might also consider signing up for my ten-month motivation reset online course. You can pay via PayPal, Zelle, or Venmo, and there are payment plans available. Let me know as soon as possible if you can do the coaching session. Okay?*

She included twelve different links to payment options for the ten-month course. I skipped over those and responded back:

> *I'll do the coaching session. I'm in. (Wait, that part's free, right?)*

After I'd responded to the email, I decided to reward myself by gathering all my past lover scarves and taking a nap under them on the couch. After all, I was about to change, and this might be the last time I let myself linger under their warmth.

After I'd shown Mira the blossoming swirls on my legs, she became overly concerned about me. She wanted to go with me everywhere—to get a latte, to my dorm room after class, to the candy store when I wanted some Swedish Fish. "It's really not that big a deal," I told her. I explained to her that several women in my family had the disease, like my mother and great-grandmother, and hadn't died from it. Yeah, my sister was dying, and my grandmother had died, sure. But that was all. It had gotten bad for them, but they were just data points. When I said this, she stared at me with the dark bullets of her eyes and shook her head.

"You're not taking this seriously. You need to tell your parents."

"They can't handle that right now. And when I'm in a neutral state, when I'm not feeling much, the swirls go away."

"We're going to go to the doctor to get it checked out."

I sighed. "Fine. If it makes you feel better."

We went to the college's health services, and the doctor pressed a long, needlelike instrument to the different spots on my legs. They only appeared because he was making me nervous with all the weird needle instruments.

"We'll have to monitor you, and you should come in for checkups every few months. But it hasn't spread to any other body parts—you're likely not in danger. Still, you'll want to tone down the emotions as you can. If it's boys that are getting you down, some of my patients have found dating reality shows to be helpful. There's one called *Circle* something. They can help introduce some numbness and desensitization to the process."

I nodded, wondering what reality dating shows he enjoyed. As I was deciding based on the splash of red in his brown hair, he held out a bowl to me. "Lollipop?" I had never had a doctor offer me a lollipop in my adulthood, but it was a nice gesture. I'd give him that.

I took one. It was purple and very sweet.

The following Friday came, and it was time for my coaching session on-air with Maisy Poppens. I'd laid out my ex-lover scarves all over the kitchen table and placed my favorite two on my lap. Scarf R smelled like eucalyptus, just like the human R.

I clicked on the Zoom link, and I was there on the screen with Maisy Poppens; I had had a dream about this very moment once. Except instead of having a human head in the dream, Maisy Poppens had an umbrella head. Anyhow, the Zoom-human-Maisy was there now, and she appeared to have freshly cut her shiny brown hair into a bob.

"I'm here today with Alia, and we're talking about her habit of hoarding ex-lover scarves and what it means to move through grief and toward growth," Maisy said. She then read my email to her, pausing dramatically after every sentence. It took six minutes for her to read through the paragraph-long message.

"So, tell us a bit more about what's been going on for you."

I tried to summate the events of the past years. "Well, my sister died when I was a senior in college, for starters," I began. "Some might say that was significant."

"I'm sensing a tone here," Maisy said, placing her finger on her nose. I had no idea what this gesture meant. "A resistance. It's common to have a defense mechanism in response to trauma."

Trauma. To have it all boiled down to the word made me feel squirmy and wrong.

I told her about the many short relationships in the aftermath. Too many to count. All of them had left me and had therefore turned into scarves. I told her about the rainbow swirls on my leg that appeared in moments of emotional intensity, that they reminded me of her. That they made all of them leave.

She nodded methodically through all my confessions. At some point, I forgot that I was confessing all of this to her on-air. To all her listeners.

"Is there someone who has seen you, all these parts of you, and stayed?"

I felt squirmy again. She wanted to see through me, and I didn't want to let her. It couldn't be this easy.

"Yes," I said. "But I pushed her away."

"Where does that resistance live in your body, Alia?"

"Nowhere," I snapped at her. At times, while listening to her podcast, her knowing tone annoyed me. But that annoyance was intensified as I looked at her face on Zoom. I wanted her questions to stop.

"Alright, sweetie. I want you to try to feel that discomfort in your body. Is it in your belly, your heart, your solar plexus?"

"What the fuck is a solar plexus?"

She didn't answer. She kept asking questions, and when I couldn't answer because my mind was frozen on an image of Mira and me, she launched into unending advice. "If it's safe, you need to find a way to reconnect with the person you pushed away, the person who saw all of you and stayed. All these scarves you're hoarding, all the memories you can't let go of—you're grasping at pieces of something that will never make you whole. The people who left you weren't meant for you. You want to be seen, but when you are seen, you shy away from it because you assume there is something about you that is unlovable."

She smiled and nodded knowingly, pushing up her glasses. I wanted to yank her glasses from her face. Why did I think this would be a good idea, being psychoanalyzed for her audience, a bunch of suburban white moms whose lives had nothing to do with mine? When I was listening to her podcast, I could imagine she was my Mary Poppins, there for me and only me. I felt the fantasy breaking.

"What have you pushed away about your sister and her death? What have you been afraid to feel?"

"I have so many feelings, I can't sell my scarves, okay? And some of them are really ugly. And some of them are from really shitty relationships. I'm not afraid to feel anything."

I felt it in my stomach, like a heavy octopus. I felt it prickling through my legs. I rolled up my pants and saw the swirls blooming.

"Thank you for your help, but I think I'm good now."

"Listen, dear Alia, I know this is too much for you, so we'll leave this here. But let me give you some advice, if you're able to listen. I want you to reach out to her, the friend you lost. I want you to sell the scarves, as much as it hurts. I want you to let in love—safe love, good love. I want you to remember your sister. Go to the places that you went to together. And see her. See the parts of her that you're afraid to see. The parts that are painful to see. Give yourself time. Be gentle with yourself. When you need someone, reach out. We're putting resources for support in the description of this video."

"Okay, thanks. Should I click End?"

"You may exit if you wish. Thank you for your vulnerability today, and for giving our listeners much to unpack. Please relish yourself."

Like a condiment? What the heck was this lady talking about? I pressed the red button, and then Zoom was frozen on her presumptuous smile, not allowing me to leave. Finally, when

I did, I let out a sigh of relief and vowed to never listen to her podcast again.

I slept in total darkness. I felt irritated when any light got into my room. And most nights, this darkness kept my mind clean, silent. But tonight I saw my sister and me at the beach, together as we'd been long ago. My little sister, younger than me and yet often seeming older than me. She carried herself like a proper adult, even at eleven. She stood on a rock. I stood next to her on another rock. The wind, fierce at this late afternoon hour, picked up her skirt, and her legs were there, bare, covered in swirls. She hadn't told anyone yet, then. But I saw, and my first instinct was to laugh.

I laughed and then snarled in disgust.

And I saw the tears inside her eyes.

I saw them pool over and fall hot on her cheeks.

I heard the boys at school making fun of her when they saw her spilling out of her jeans.

I heard their screeching laughter.

I saw our mother and father fighting about coming to this country, wanting to leave. I saw where their screams lived inside her body.

I saw everything she felt, and I looked away.

In college, I undressed in my dorm room before a dance, and Mira was with me. I never knew what to wear for school dances, especially one that was called “Senior Screw.” So Mira gave me one of her dresses, a dark red lace one, which was a little too big for me and rested right above my knees.

“Is it too short? I can’t reach the zipper in the back.”

“Here, I’ll do it for you.” She touched my shoulders, and her touch sent shivers down my body to my legs.

I didn’t say anything, but Mira saw me staring at my legs. It didn’t happen unless I was feeling more than I could say.

“What are you feeling?” she asked me, holding my face.

I felt her love for me, and it overwhelmed me. I felt my love for her, the colors of it, the way it would overwhelm her if she truly knew its contents. The love swirled and contorted into something monstrous; it congealed and became bumpy and ugly. I didn’t want it to be mine.

So I expelled it. I pushed her away. I didn’t want her to touch me, to feel this ugliness rising within me.

So I ran away to Haystack Rock.

So I told her to leave.

So I sat on the floor of my dorm room in the red pool of her dress.

So I loved someone, then I loved someone else, and I collected the scarves of them.

It was natural to leave when you saw what someone was truly made of.

When you couldn’t bear the shades of their emotions.

I didn’t believe that Mira could bear them, so I made her go.

I left myself too.

Six months had passed since my disastrous conversation with Maisy Poppens. I never responded to her email requesting an update on my progress for her listeners.

But I did eventually email the residents in my apartment complex to set a time for my scarf sale. "It's gonna be a big one," I wrote. "This is the first time I've ever done this. Yes, I know you're supposed to sell your scarves every year. I just took a little longer (my whole life). There will be an eclectic mix of scarves: infinity, satin, silk. Take your pick."

It was a big affair. People I'd never seen before showed up, including some guy in a huge red top hat. I wasn't sure if he even lived in the building. But how would I know anyway? Since I'd been cycling through a string of relationships, then confined in my self-help podcast cave, I hadn't really met anyone who lived here.

Should I have told the buyers of my scarves the stories of the relationships they belonged to? Maybe, but I wanted them to have new stories. To gain new sentience in the lives of others.

I had felt so angry at Maisy Poppens since our conversation—for her presumptuousness, for the advice I had sought but didn't want to receive. I had written drafted emails to her, detailing my frustrations with her comments, refuting her diagnoses of me. But I never sent those emails.

But last week, I went to the doctor for a checkup, and I told them about the swirls on my legs. They said I was still safe, but I had to come in every month to monitor it. I nodded. This time, I would do so. This time, I would stop shielding myself with scarves of lovers gone. Holding on to remnants of them would not make them come back. That wasn't what I wanted anyway.

I wanted *them* to come back. My grandmother, my sister, my mom. My mother wasn't gone, not dead, but she wasn't living either. She sat suspended in her room, waiting for her mother and daughter. My grandmother and sister were gone, and I was there when they both died in the same way, like broken dams, waves rushing from them.

Could I have lingered in their oceans? Could I have danced in the light of their rainbows?

I remember running instead, down the hallways of the hospitals, where the water from their bodies rushed after me, clinging to my ankles. What was eerie was the beauty of it all. I had never seen the world so full of color, a hospital so achingly alive.

If I was going to go the same way, if this was our story, I decided I wanted to be alive in the world while I was here.

So I had to sell all my scarves.

I watched as people walked away with my scarves, smiling. An older lady who had somehow obtained a name tag—her name was Becky, apparently—got the infinity scarf (A). The red-top-hat man got N, emerald green silk. And in the mix of faces I didn't recognize was someone I thought I'd seen before.

She wandered, looking confused, holding up an umbrella even though it was forecasted to be sunny without a drop of rain all day. Mary Poppins? I wondered. No, no. Her hair was short and straight, jet black, and she was wearing the dress I'd worn to Senior Screw. And Nike tennis shoes alongside the elegant red lace of her dress. Everything about her seemed out of place. Everything about her seemed like Mira, but it couldn't be her. I had checked her social media. She lived in Baltimore for graduate school. Still, I felt like I knew her. She was some version of Mira, a collage of every vision I'd had of her since we last spoke.

I'd always wanted to see her again. I wanted to eat ice cream with her, to pretend to run with her, to see her hair. But the years had compounded, and my silence had hardened; I figured she wouldn't want to hear from me. Who would want to hear from a person who'd disappeared like I had?

Since I'd talked with Maisy Poppens, I dreamt of her every single night. In every dream, she was wearing the red lace dress, even though I'd never actually seen her in it. I was the only one who'd worn it.

She smiled a half smile, and when the sale was done, when all my scarves were gone, living on others' bodies, I followed her, Mira-but-not-Mira. She knew something that I did not. She led me back to my apartment, and we didn't talk. She kept smiling, and I believed in the truth of her, though it made no sense. She knocked on my door, and I unlocked it.

Inside, it looked so bare. I walked to the kitchen, where Scarf N had been, and the living room, where scarves had resided in a pile. All of it was gone. Alarm rose in my belly, but Mira-but-not-Mira held me. I didn't even feel her through the shock of the nothingness. I wanted to cry, but nothing came out.

"You didn't want a scarf?" I asked Mira-but-not-Mira. She shook her head no but still didn't say a word. I had so much to say to her, but words could not contain what we were saying to each other now.

She enfolded me in her own silence, and I felt safe in the home she made. She led me to the closet where I kept my sister as a quilt.

I picked my sister up for the first time in years. We walked to the couch. I walked carefully, holding my quilt-sister tightly.

I cradled her, seeing all her vibrancy, the blue and red and yellow and orange, the endless swirls on the fabric. I unfolded her and placed her on my knees. Underneath her quilt, my own swirls blossomed. Mira-but-not-Mira pressed each swirl, and I felt a sharp pang each time. I saw my sister in front of the mirror at home long ago.

She wasn't mad at me for my leaving. She knew I was returning now.

I placed the quilt over Mira-not-Mira's body. I let her rest under it with me. It couldn't cover both of our legs. I held Mira-but-not-Mira, running my hands through her hair.

She looked at me. My legs, my cheeks, my lips. Everything turning to rainbow. *It was too much and congealed into something ugly, ugly, ugly—*

I let her see.

I let myself feel what I was becoming.

KEROSENE

THE SKY IN OREGON blazed orange. Priya looked outside and thought of her mother's kerosene lamp burning on through the night's darkness. In India, she kept it on her nightstand and left it on when Priya's father was out late at the neighbors' house, chattering away. Priya could hear the whispers of their voices and the silence in her own house. Her mother left her door ajar, and the light spilled into young Priya's room. Priya craved this light, its burning glow.

The sky glowed with an eerie beauty. Priya and her daughter sat watching the news. Lightning had ignited the wildfire that spread over the state. Their belongings were packed up in suitcases. They were on a Level 1 evacuation warning now, and Deepak was on the line. He was watching the news too. He had accrued hotel points from his frequent work travels to California and said they should use some and go.

Rohisha sat far away from Priya, on the other side of the couch. They'd spent several weekends together like this when Deepak was away for work trips. A wall remained between them; Rohisha stared at Priya, her eyes like dark marbles.

"When is Dad home?" she asked. Priya ignored the question.

"Did you put the clothes you might need in your suitcase?" she asked her twelve-year-old.

When the news issued a Level 2 evacuation for the area, Priya decided they would go. She looked at the backyard, the skeletal branches of trees dancing in their ethereal surroundings. She stared at the whole mess of the branches and imagined them catapulted into a fire. What would happen if it all went away like that, in a flash? She thought of her mother's lamp, the flickering brightness.

"Should I get in the car?"

"Yes. Go now. I'll be right there."

Deepak had booked a room at a Hampton Inn in Hillsboro. As she drove the Jeep down the highway, she thought about the sky in different areas of Portland and in downtown, where the family would go to the Saturday Market. She remembered the time she bought Rohisha spoon- and-fork-shaped earrings. This had made Rohisha happy. She stopped wearing earrings soon after, her skin drying around her ears from swimming.

In their hotel room, Priya and Rohisha sat across from each other on separate beds. Rohisha pressed her knees together, sitting up tall. When she was Rohisha's age, Priya suffered from bad posture.

Her mother had no problem pointing this out to her again and again. She thought about telling Rohisha but refrained.

"Should we go and find somewhere to eat?"

"It's 4:30."

"Well, do you want to turn on the TV? See what channels they have here?"

"It's always *Big Bang Theory*. I hate that show."

"Why?"

"The Indian guy's a stereotype."

Priya smiled because she admired so deeply how her daughter spoke her mind. She loved Rohisha's wit, her sarcasm, that all of her emotions, even if she tried to hide them, appeared in plain sight on her face.

"You're laughing at me."

"I'm not."

Rohisha turned on the TV. On the news, Priya saw the smoke rising all over town.

"Will our house get destroyed?" Rohisha asked. She lay down on the bed, her curly hair splayed out.

"No, no, nothing like that. The smoke is just dangerous for us to be around."

Rohisha and Deepak suffered from asthma. Priya dusted the house several times a week, and around Rohisha's bed frame so nothing triggering would get into her body.

Rohisha was typing something on her flip phone. Priya wondered who her daughter texted. Deepak texted Priya: *You both try to get some rest, get some food.*

When they walked out, Priya smelled the smoke, though it was less intense than in the suburbs. It still made Rohisha cough, and Priya rubbed her daughter's back, but Rohisha flinched, pushing her away. They walked from restaurant to restaurant—an Italian place, a Moroccan place, Subway—and all were closed. An Indian restaurant was open. "How about here?" Priya asked. "You like butter chicken."

"It's been forever since I've liked that," Rohisha said. "I hate those creamy sauces." She didn't eat Priya's South Indian food either; once upon a time, she liked the okra curry she used to make. She remembered making dosa after dosa and Rohisha sitting on her stool, poking holes in the middle of the round dough and begging for more. What had happened to that child who used to be so hungry for many things?

The hotel restaurant was open, and Rohisha ordered a chicken and basil dish. She and Deepak ate meat, though Priya wished they didn't. It wasn't just about Hinduism or what their relatives would think; the thought of meat, its texture—which she imagined as slimy since she'd seen a raw piece of chicken—disgusted her.

Though her daughter was not talking to her, Priya enjoyed the peaceful silence. Rohisha ate quickly, gulping each bite down so fast she didn't seem to be tasting the food. Then her face grew a reddish hue and her lips bulged out slightly, and she looked at Priya.

"What's wrong?"

Rohisha pointed wordlessly at her plate, then spit out what she had chewed. Priya saw the greenish part of the mixture and understood. Rohisha had eaten pesto, which must've had pine nuts in it. Priya didn't have the bag with the EpiPen and the Benadryl. "Let's go upstairs," she told her daughter. "Can you breathe?"

Rohisha nodded. Priya held her daughter's hand and Rohisha rose. She waved to the waiter and paid. This hadn't happened for some time now—maybe a year or so. Priya felt like it was her fault somehow. If Deepak were here, it wouldn't have happened.

She patted Rohisha's back and held her hand tightly. This time, Rohisha didn't let go.

In the room, after taking Benadryl, Rohisha lay on her bed. Priya watched her, her hair all over the pillow, eyes closed, her mouth open. Priya felt the urge to describe how her daughter looked right then, how her image transported Priya across the planes of time. She knew Rohisha didn't want to be seen like Priya saw her, as a child, but what else could her daughter be to her? She remembered when they'd found out Rohisha was allergic to nuts. Deepak had fed her a walnut, and then they were in the hospital, Rohisha's lips red blossoms. "She's brave," the doctor had said, poking all over her arm to test for allergies. "A brave trooper, this one."

Priya watched the news on silent. The same images—the bright orange sky, embers of smoke. She turned it off. She moved to Rohisha's bed, trying not to make sounds as she adjusted her body. She saw the hotel notepad on the bedside table. She brought it to her lap and began to write.

> *Her hair, wisps of clouds. The pink sky rising, citrus sting. Her lips as she'd been that day, long ago. I ran home from the store so quickly, cereal box in hand. Ran home to my daughter.*

Priya was embarrassed by her overwrought descriptions. She swore that, once, she could write. But the feeling that was central to her writing, the emotion that used to overflow before she was married to Deepak, had withered. It felt forced. She used to hear something, a rhythm, within her. It was gone now. Sometimes, the role of mother to her felt like a part, something she'd slipped into without quite knowing why. She loved this child. She just couldn't quite find the words for that love.

Perhaps this was how her mother had felt. She remembered the many evenings of kneading phulka dough alone, trying to concoct songs in her head to keep her company. All those times, while the chatter roared on in the living room, Priya's mother was sleeping. Priya felt it too, this urge to sleep on and on, to crawl into an abyss away from motherhood, from being a wife, a daughter.

Rohisha moved, grabbing Priya's thigh. It was an awkward place to grab, and it confirmed Priya's thought that her daughter was still deep in Benadryl-inspired dreamland. But a few moments later, she rose, still bleary-eyed but awake.

"What happened, Mari?"

She had her earphones in; Priya hadn't noticed before. She fiddled with them, pulling them out of her ears and putting them back in. "Can you hear anything?" Rohisha asked. Then she asked why it was so hot.

"I can see if I can turn down the heat."

"I'm so tired," she said.

"Here, some water," Priya said, filling a cup from the sink. "Do you need more medicine?"

"No, it knocked me out. There's still a little pain in my throat."

"I can make you some tea."

"I don't want that." She drank a sip of water. She drank slowly, and her words came out even slower. "I want my face to not have to be fixed."

"What're you talking about?"

"That's what Kyle Anderson said."

"What? When did he say that?"

"When we were doing our projects in computer lab about what we were going to do when we grow up."

"Who is he to say that? Let me talk to his parents." Suddenly, the Priya who had stayed away from PTA meetings all of Rohisha's schooling years, away from the Blossom Grove parents, was ready to face Kyle Anderson's entitled parents. She became, like many mothers, a fierce hen when it came to her daughter.

"Don't do that. He swims with me." She had a worried look on her face that made Priya's heart sink. "You know my friend Tara? She eats asparagus and chicken every night."

"What we eat is fine. Keeps you strong."

Rohisha sank back into the bedsheets. "The chlorine makes my skin dry. The dermatologist said if you had dry skin, you won't have acne, but that's not true. Our family has all the skin issues. I have a bad genetic code."

"That's not true. We have good genetics. So many smart people in your family, like your dad and my mother . . ."

"I don't know anything about Ajji. I never have anything to say to her on the phone."

Rohisha shut her eyes again. She collapsed into the powerful embrace of sleep.

What had Priya really said to her mother all those years growing up? The most she understood of her was through the flickering lamplight, the flashing signal. On always when Priya's father was out, but through the day, she acted indifferent to him. At night, when he wasn't there, the light cried out. Absence. Absence. The word crawled across the floor. Priya remembered the rustling when her father returned, sometimes at 1:00, 2:00 a.m., and moments before he entered, her mother's scurrying around like an animal. She turned off the light. So that Priya's father would never know how much she needed him.

One night, when she was eleven years old, Priya, having had a bad dream—one about jalebi-eating monsters, their mouths awash in a tacky orange glow—tiptoed across to her mother's room. She stopped in the living room, hesitant, afraid. She saw her mother's head, could smell, so close, the coconut oil in her hair. She stood in her mother's room, a golden hue of light reaching her mother's toes, making them, in their discoloration, strangely beautiful.

She lay down next to her mother, making a pillow with her hands. Her mother moved toward Priya, giving her a bit of her shawl. She placed her arm over Priya, and Priya could feel what linked the two of them together.

"I'm hungry," Rohisha said, and so Priya ordered from the hotel restaurant again. She got what Rohisha loved: carbonara pasta. She wondered if it was a good idea, Rohisha eating so heavily when she'd just recovered from her allergies, but she wanted her daughter to be happy, even fleetingly.

Rohisha heaped the pasta onto her fork and swallowed quickly. The medicine had made her hungry. But then her stomach hurt and she ran to the bathroom. "It's hard to breathe," she said, and Priya followed her in.

She searched in the bag for the inhaler, but, panicking, she couldn't find it. She called Deepak, but the call didn't go through.

He struggled with asthma, and he'd be able to give her instructions. The Wi-Fi wasn't connected. She called him on WhatsApp. It sounded like he was eating something. "What happened?"

"Where's the inhaler? Rohisha's having trouble breathing."

"The front pocket of the backpack." It was an intuitive place, but with him telling her, she found it. Rohisha inhaled, breathing in the medicine. Priya smelled the metallic scent of the inhaler and encouraged her daughter to keep breathing. In, out. In, out.

"*Ēnāyitu?*" She heard the voice coming from her phone. "What happened?" Priya's mother asked.

Her face was on Priya's screen. She'd hung up on Deepak and clicked somehow on her mother's name. Her mother, 8,197 miles away, stared straight at her. Many mornings this week, her mother had sent Priya her routine *Good morning* message with big, sprawling white text on the background of a golden Ganesha. Priya hadn't responded. She felt a pang of guilt about this now.

"Amma, what're you doing up? It's very early there."

"I get up before your appa now. Drink coffee. Listen to birds. It is peaceful."

For as long as Priya had lived with her mother, she'd never known her to get up early. She'd known her, in fact, for days, to not get up at all. Priya hadn't called her in a few weeks. Priya found that as the guilt of distance filled her, piled up within her, she avoided the calls more. The silence between them festered into a bruise.

"Sometimes I walk," her mother continued in Kannada. "You know they've made a new park? I take circles around the monuments there."

"That's very nice, Amma. Rohisha's struggling a bit now—can I call you back?" Rohisha was bent over the sink, taking in gulps of air. Priya could see her eyes in the mirror; she looked at Priya like she wanted her to disappear.

"You're okay, Jaanmari?"

"Fine," Rohisha said shakily. "You can talk to Ajji."

Priya sat on the bed, watching her daughter. She spoke quietly. "Rohisha ate some nuts and had allergies, and I think she's panicking too. So her asthma is flaring up. Deepak is in California, and we had to evacuate our home and come to a hotel because of the wildfires. Rohisha told me," Priya said, her voice a near whisper, "that some boy at school told her she needs to fix her face. How can a kid be so cruel?"

"I can hear you!" Rohisha walked out of the bathroom, hands balled into fists. Priya couldn't tell what she was fighting. "This is why I don't want to tell you things. You just tell everybody." She was getting worked up, like she used to when she was even younger. The last time Priya's mother had visited Oregon, Rohisha was going through "a phase of fury," as she and Deepak had termed it. This was a few years ago—she was nine then—and she often balled her hands into fists like this when she didn't like the answers, the way things were.

She'd slam the door to her room and sit at the windowsill, making herself as small as could be. She'd wait for someone to enter her room, to come looking for her, but it had to be the right person. Priya wasn't the right person. When Priya's mother was visiting, Rohisha accepted her. This had annoyed Priya. Once, Priya stood just outside Rohisha's door, looking in as her mother spoon-fed Rohisha dal and rice. This was all she had to do?

"Here, eat hot food, you feel better," she said. She didn't have to say anything else. Rohisha swallowed quietly. Rohisha had been wearing a sun-bright yellow dress. She stared at this woman who shared her lineage, someone she did not really know and yet the only person who could comfort her daughter through her simple silence.

Clenching her teeth now, perhaps because she didn't know what else to do, Rohisha turned off all the lights. She stood in the darkness, a small shadowy figure, swaying. She cried loudly, like a child vying for attention, but Priya knew that anything she did would upset her. "Come, sit here. Just breathe."

Priya's mother gestured over the video call. "She can talk to me," she told Priya.

Rohisha took the phone.

"What's wrong, Mari?" her ajji asked.

"I can't breathe. And Mom said all those things."

"She didn't mean anything by it," Priya's mother said. Rohisha ran back into the bathroom, the door shutting behind her, but then she opened it, leaving it ajar.

"She cares for you," Ajji said. Rohisha's sobs softened. Now Priya was grateful for her mother's words. She did know just what to say, even if she hadn't known when Priya was a child.

"Look at me," Ajji said. "Look up. Your mother is not only my child; you are my child too. Do you hear me? I see you on the screen. Your hair, so full, so beautiful. Your eyes are shining."

"I'm crying."

"Doesn't matter. They shine all the time. Bright. Like your mother's."

Rohisha sat in the bathroom for a while, and after some time, her breathing seemed to regularize.

She spoke softly. "Good night, Ajji. Thanks."

Priya's eyes were closing, but she wanted to be awake as long as her daughter was. Sometime later, when she had waded in and out of sleep, she saw her daughter standing above her and felt her small hand on her cheek. Rohisha touched her own face after. Then she turned on the light in the bathroom. Neither of them could sleep in the dark.

IN LAMPLIGHT YOU ARE MADE WHOLE

CHAYA FELL SILENT WHEN her mother died. After the funeral and the grimaced smiles and convoluted paperwork, Chaya walked to the market and bought a handful of okra. She used her pointer finger to speak. She was tired of the noisy words. She returned to her apartment at the edge of the loud city and buried herself under a sea of white blankets. After a restless, dreamless sleep, Chaya crawled out from under the blankets and emerged into the living room. By the window, a gleaming easel had appeared, along with a blank canvas that stared directly at her. Chaya moved hypnotically toward it, picking up the wide paintbrush on the easel. She brushed it, bare, across the canvas. She then dipped the brush in the pool of dark paint that bloomed on the coffee table and brought it back to the canvas, and a picture started to emerge.

She would make a portrait of her mother shrouded in darkness, holding a clay oil lamp. When Chaya closed her eyes, she could see the full image, the jellyfish-like light patterning the space around her mother's head, her free arm reaching out, as if to Chaya, beyond the frame. In her vision, her mother's hand covered Chaya's face, blocking any sound from coming out.

Each morning, she woke and stood by the canvas, and her hand seemed to know how to curve, to contort, to move the picture from her mind onto the page. She took short breaks only to pace fourteen times around the easel, return circulation to her legs, or eat steaming dal and rice cross-legged on the floor. Large peppercorns swam whole in the dal soup, and they lodged in her throat, and she would cough, angry not that she was coughing but that the whole ordeal was taking her away from her painting.

Before he went off to work at the local bank, Chaya's husband would wave her goodbye, asking no questions about her silence. Chaya assumed that he welcomed it—the silence—because it meant she bothered him less with details of her day and queries about his. Before her silence, Chaya noted his noncommittal grunts and nods in response to her recounting her walks around the neighborhood, the sunbirds she saw flocking around the pond like moths to light. She watched him take out his cigar as she was speaking and step out onto the porch, smoke slithering from between his lips. He fiddled with his phone. She assumed he'd been sleeping with Jaya, a coworker, for some time now. It no longer caused her pain—the image of them entangled—Rajiv swirling his tongue around Jaya's nipples, her moaning in pleasure. Rather, when such images intruded, she waved them away, irritated by the distraction from her painting, from the recreation of her mother.

After Rajiv left, she could embed herself deeply into the portrait, rendering the gold embroidery of her mother's sari, the copper-like hue of the lamplight spreading thickly over the dark. As she painted each detail—a fold in the sari, the shape of her mother's eyelids—memories returned to her. Her mother sitting on the porch steps in their red house in Bangalore, hands placed over her knees, watching the neighbor's dog twist endlessly in a patch of sun. Standing in the doorway to the kitchen, silent as young Chaya stood before her, urging her to speak, to tell her father it wasn't fair he wasn't letting Chaya play with her friend. *Girls*, he said, *shouldn't let themselves loose in the world*. Pursing her lips, knitting in the bedroom as Chaya's father stood outside, hurling insults like tiny knives. *Why won't you speak!* Chaya had yelled in frustration, and her mother stared at her with a tiny, lopsided smile, eyes stoic and shining, and now, in the renewed clarity of memory, Chaya recognized the hurt that glistened in her mother's eyes then, in her woven-together lips sealed shut so the world would never hear the lilt of the syllables caught in her mouth.

Twenty-seven days after she began the portrait, Chaya finished. A shock ran through her spine one morning when she saw that she needed just one more brush of gold on her mother's forehead. She pulled the brush across her mother's skin until it glistened, then Chaya fell back, dropping her paintbrush on the floor, and the clattering sound rippled across her face and ears, and her mother loomed large in front of her, full of flesh and golden light, and still her mother stood distant, still she moved away, until her eyes softened and she welcomed Chaya into her arms, and in the wake of the embrace, Chaya touched her mother's mouth, and then it all fell out, all the words she'd kept inside, all she'd never been able to tell her, and as the words fell to the ground, they shimmered like light, quick bells, growing faster until they surrounded her, making a song only Chaya could hear, a song that had lived starving inside her mother so long.

A SWEATER FOR YOU

IT IS A TERRIFYING thing to lose your body, I thought, as my son Srinivas knelt before my feet. He was scrubbing my toes because I had become useless and could not wash my own feet. My body had become useless. The gold ring around my big toe had faded over time. My husband, Keshav, bought it for me when we first married. Those days were still vivid to me, though he was gone now and I was no longer young. I tried not to think too much of those days. They were gone, like the dirt from my feet down the drain.

Srinivas and Lakshmi took me to the park today. We sat by the pond and threw strips of white bread into the water. I hadn't the energy to tear the bread, so Srinivas did it for me. It gleamed like fresh milk, ribbons of floating flour. I started to feel tired not fifteen minutes into the outing. I could feel my fatigue weighing Srinivas and Lakshmi down. They'd not been out of the house in a while because of me. I felt I had imprisoned them here, made them stay with my sickness. But it was unbearable before Srinivas arrived. I could not stand it, to see myself and only myself in the mirror each morning. The cups and plates gathered in the room Keshav and I used to sleep in together. All I did was make coffee again and again, even at night. Sometimes I ate bare slices of bread. Or I'd cut a packet of milk and watch it plop, plop, plop into the pot. Once, I turned on the burner and left it on. I went to sleep, and Sowmya from next door smelled the smoke. I didn't know what would've happened if she hadn't. Sometimes I dreamed it raged on, the burner, and I was sleeping under my blankets, which wrapped tight around me, nearly choking me. In the dream, I couldn't release myself from them even though I smelled the burning. The smoke crept from the kitchen to the bedroom, but I was chained to the bed, and the smoke grew and I was coughing and coughing and then Keshav covered my mouth, covered it so hard that, under the smoke and blankets, I stopped breathing altogether.

I didn't tell Srinivas about these dreams, and his brother, Karthik, barely called anymore, so I didn't tell him either. When I messaged Karthik on WhatsApp, I received only a few words in response. *Busy now amma , Ananya has recital .will call later.* Most days, he never called.

One morning, I was trying to call him and he didn't pick up. That morning—a rarity since Keshav had died—I felt like eating. The guavas on the tree outside had begun to ripen, and their bright green bodies reminded me of Karthik and Srinivas's childhood, when the boys would race each other up the tree to the terrace. I walked outside to pick some fruit and saw a beautiful glistening guava up on the branches. I reached for it but missed it, even on my tiptoes. Then I reached further, and the next thing I knew, I was on my back on the hard ground.

I tried to move, but each miniscule motion felt like burning needles thrashing through my spine. I stayed on the ground for some time, until the spring heat subsided and wind brushed through the trees and the crickets began to sing their monotonous song. I somehow made my way back into the house slowly, holding on to my hip the whole fourteen steps inside, then collapsed on the cot and stayed there for the rest of the night. When I woke, I called Srinivas and told him what happened. He had become my reliable son. "I'll come, Amma, I'll find a way to get a week off work, I can come, don't worry." He had stayed for months now; his job allowed him to work remotely. I wished for him to be selfish like his brother, to not leave his family for me, but if he hadn't, I might have been dead, and I suppose somewhere inside, I still wanted to live.

It had been a week since the hip replacement surgery. The recovery had been slow. Now, Srinivas rubbed calamine lotion on my feet. "Your feet have become very cracked," he said. His feet had been cracked like this too when he was a child. I used to rub calamine lotion all over them for weeks, months, after he would go and play in the cricket field with his friends.

I've become you as a child, I thought, but the words slipped out of my mouth. I didn't speak much these days because most of what I said was interpreted by Srinivas as a cry for help. I must have seemed too crazy or sick to say anything normal.

"What, Amma?" His eyes widened.

I said nothing, knitted my lips together tight. He went back to scrubbing the lotion on my feet.

As Srinivas grew older, he spent his days trying to get away from the house and his father. I understood his impulse, though I would never say it out loud. Karthik was often at school late, studying or meeting with his professor, so I would be left alone to the house with Keshav. He spent the latter half of the day drawing diagrams of parts of computers on a large sketch pad, and during these hours, he didn't want to be bothered, but he needed to be fed. I would whip up large pots of sambar and steaming rice and bring them to him at the dining table, where he'd sit staring at a large canvas of paper, not looking up at me. Many days, I felt merely like his servant, not his wife.

Now the past wrapped around my ankles like a bracelet inextricable from skin.

"Amma, here, sit on this stool." Srinivas began to dry my feet with a washcloth. Lakshmi hovered outside the bathroom. When I looked at the two of them now, I felt responsible for the intertwined sorrows of their lives. In his childhood, I never stood up for Srinivas. He was the sensitive child, and what good was sensitivity in the world?

He stood before me, holding my hands as I rose from the stool, and I could see the sensitivity in his face. He had become angrier later on, I knew—but I still saw him for his kindness, for the light that radiated at the brown centers of his eyes.

I must have started mouthing words because he called Lakshmi into the bathroom, and they both stared at me like a spectacle.

"What is she trying to say?" Srinivas turned to Lakshmi. Communication passed between them like I wasn't there.

My hearing aid had lost some battery, but I didn't want to tell Srinivas. I had the sense that if I heard everything they said about me, the knowledge would hurt me.

I couldn't hear much of the world around me, but I could always hear my dead brother Rajan's voice resounding in my ears. At night, his whispers grew into a scream. Rajan had died in an auto rickshaw accident. The news report said that the auto rickshaw driver had been drunk, but he didn't die. Only Rajan. Rajan was going back home to his wife, Neha, and four-month-old baby, Durga. Sometimes I imagined Durga's cries when she understood her father was never coming back home. Sometimes I imagined Neha cradling Durga, rocking her back and forth, standing at the door of their house and waiting for Rajan, who would never come.

One night, near the beginning of Keshav's anger, he found me in our room where I was knitting a yellow baby's sweater. I was knitting it for Durga, who had grown by then into an eight-year-old. I knitted it for the idea I had of her; I hadn't seen her since she was a child. Keshav sat next to me on the bed and stared at my hands as I moved the needle through the yarn.

"Who are you making this for?"

"Sowmya's new baby," I lied.

He clasped my chin and pulled my head up to meet his eyes. "You're always hiding behind that yarn of yours."

"Just making a sweater to be nice."

"It's not for her baby, is it? It's for that Durga still."

I could see the anger rising in his eyes, so I stayed silent. I slowly returned to the knitting. He yanked the yarn from my hands.

"When will you get over your brother and be here, in our life?" He held the back of my head as he said this, spit oozing out his mouth as he became more animated. It felt like a strange accusation for him to make when he spent hours each day buried in his diagrams, paying no attention to Srinivas, who he saw as weaker than Karthik.

"I *am* here," I said, though I knew there was truth to his words. I wasn't fully there, since half of me still existed with Rajan.

"Good," he said and brushed a strand of my hair over my ear. He kissed my forehead and pressed my body to the bed. I could tell he wanted something, so I opened my legs and wrapped them around his hips. He began to move into me, and I let it happen.

We had been inseparable, my brother Rajan and me. We slept in the same room on bunk beds until our teenage years, and in that shared space, we would narrate our days to each other, and whatever had happened in them, good or bad, became alright. I would tell him about the girl in my upper-primary class who spoke like she was the teacher, judging the quality of everyone else's comments, and he, only a few months older than me, would tell me about his biology teacher, who would bring samosas to class and barely teach them anything. We were each other's confidants until the year before secondary school, when our parents sat us down and told us that they could afford to send only one of us to an English-medium school. They didn't tell us this explicitly, but we both knew who it would be; we both knew that the education system valued boys' minds over girls', that it would be Rajan who would go on to study and attend graduate school and become an engineer while I would become a housewife. It was just the way things were.

That summer, before Rajan began school at St. Philomena, he started hanging out with Tejas, the boy across the street. Tejas would also be attending St. Philomena and lived in the biggest house in the neighborhood, which held an expansive book collection and a large, spiraling staircase, like the ones found in ballrooms. Sometimes, coming back home from school, I would linger outside of the house and peer inside, watching Tejas's mother and father sitting at their dining table, and their lives would seem like something I could never reach.

As Rajan grew closer to Tejas, he became quieter at night, revealing fewer and fewer details about his day. One evening, he asked our parents if he could start sleeping in the spare room. Since he was about to start secondary school, he said, he needed some independence, and they agreed. I suspected that, somehow, Tejas was taking my brother away from me. Some days, he would return home in the late afternoons, smelling like smoke. He'd run to the bathroom and scrub his body clean for dinner so our parents wouldn't notice anything.

One night, he came from the spare room into my room. He stood by the door and spoke in a hushed voice.

"Mamatha, are you sleeping?" he asked.

I rose and sat up on the bed. I was on the top bunk. "What is it?"

"I've been smoking with Tejas," he whispered. "I know you know. Don't you dare tell Amma and Appa."

The look in his eyes scared me. He seemed suddenly not like my brother but someone foreign to me. "I won't," I said.

"On Friday, Amma and Appa are going to the temple for puja. They'll be gone most of the afternoon. Tejas and some other boys from St. Philomena are going to come over, and there'll be smoking and drinking. I'm just telling you now so you aren't surprised to see them."

He spoke to me as though I were a barrier to his enjoyment, someone to deal with so he could go on and live his life. I couldn't understand it, this sudden transformation in my brother, his desire to belong to anyone but me.

After that Friday night, the shape of my world changed. My brother, Tejas, and Rahul tried unsuccessfully to rid the house of the pot-smoke smell with Amma's perfumes and air fresheners. When Appa entered the house, I could see that he knew immediately someone else had been there. He walked to the cot and examined it, bending to find a flannel shirt stuffed in its corner, one that Rahul had left behind. Rajan stood watching Appa as Appa brought the shirt to his nose and sniffed.

"Smell this," he said, squinting at Rajan, then turning to give the shirt to Amma. "Smell, and tell me what you think it is."

Amma sniffed at it and didn't say anything but stared with creased brows at Rajan. Rajan turned to look at me, as if trying to find in my face the answer to his conundrum.

"Whose shirt is this?" Appa asked Rajan, walking toward him. I observed the stark difference in their heights. "Whose shirt is it?"

Rajan hung his head and didn't look up at Appa for a while. Then he turned back to me again. I didn't know what he was looking at me for. "Mamatha invited a school friend over, and they were smoking," Rajan said, his voice unfaltering. I could hardly believe what he said. I thought it must've been some cruel joke, that he'd start laughing any minute and tell Appa that it had actually been his doing.

Appa walked to me. Amma stayed transfixed at the other end of the room. He held the shirt to my nose. "Which friend of yours?"

I looked at Rajan. I didn't know what to say. I only ever spent time with my classmate Tanvi outside of classes; we went to the movie theater in Koramangala sometimes, catching the newest Raj Kapoor films.

"It's a boy's," Rajan said.

"A boy?" Appa looked me up and down.

"Someone you don't know," I said. I didn't know why I was playing along. Somewhere inside, I suppose I still wanted Rajan to love me.

"What's his name?"

"Lakshman," I said. I didn't know any Lakshmans at school, so I hoped Appa wouldn't be able to track one down.

"Well," he said, moving over to the cot and sitting down. "I'm very disappointed in *both* of you that you would misuse our prayer time like this. But I'm especially disappointed in you, Mamatha." I felt my legs weakening, my heartbeat quickening. "I never expected this of you."

That night, I slept restlessly. The rims of my eyes burned, and my head softly throbbed. I heard the door opening, and when I sat up, I saw Rajan standing there.

"I'm sorry, Mamatha," he whispered. I didn't want to talk to him. "It just came out."

I glared at him.

"But you know it makes more sense." He walked to the center of the bedroom and squinted up at me. "I mean, they're sending me to St. Philomena. That's how it was always going to be." I could hear what he was not saying, the chorus that thrummed beneath his words. *Your future doesn't matter as much as mine.* "It isn't personal. It just seemed like the way to lose the least."

I lost many things that day. My parents told me I had to clean the house all summer, every inch of it, the base of the toilet and the pots and pans, the residue of dirt and grime. *Scrub until you bleed*, my appa said. He wanted to scrub all the disobedience out of me. I had to clean Rajan's room, every corner of it, while Rajan waited outside and watched. I tidied his school papers, arranged them neatly on his new desk, seeing the English words that populated the pages, unable to read any of them.

In the years that followed, Rajan graduated with his master's in computer science, found a job at Infosys, and married Neha, Tejas's younger sister. I only finished two years of secondary school, then committed myself fully to housework as Amma and Appa tried to find me a husband.

I still remembered the ache of one morning, before I married Keshav. My amma, standing in the bathroom, door ajar, spoke to me. I stood in the kitchen, watching her brush her hair as she always did, violently twisting out the knots and tangles with the spine of her comb. She rubbed coconut oil from a small blue bottle between her palms and spread it all over her scalp so her hair glistened, a pool of shimmering black. "She is so beautiful, no?" She spoke about Neha, Rajan's then fiancée. "And so fair."

One night, when Rajan was out buying milk at the market, I stole the picture of Neha from his desk. The photo was printed on a shiny piece of paper, showing Neha's light brown skin, a shade that resembled caramel before it burned in a saucepan. I walked to the bathroom and locked the door, holding the photo of Neha up next to my face. Her skin was at least two shades lighter than mine. I touched my skin, which was dark brown and ruptured with the aftermath of acne. I took a tube of the Fair & Lovely cream my mother had brought me from the store and squeezed out three-fourths of it into my palm. I lathered the cream on my face, and it burned on the acne sores. I left it there for minutes, staring at my cream-colored face. Under the prescribed whiteness, where all of my features were hidden, I felt safe. My ugliness, my darkness, was hidden. Then, after the cream had hardened into a paste, I ran my hands under sink water and brought a washcloth to my face. I heard my appa's voice, telling me to *scrub, scrub, scrub* under the sink, under the toilet, to wipe away all the dust and dirt. I scrubbed, scrubbed, scrubbed at my skin until the dormant acne broke out into pools of pus, and pins of blood erupted all over the terrain of my cheeks, and I wanted to scream from the pain, but I didn't. I looked down at the picture of Neha. Droplets of my blood scattered across her face; it was as though, for an instant, we were intertwined, as though I were beautiful too.

"Scrub, scrub," I said out loud in the bathroom now, and Srinivas looked at Lakshmi. She walked into the shower, where I was, and held my hand.

"You okay, Amma?"

I nodded.

"We finished cleaning your feet," Srinivas said. "All done now."

It struck me how, when you got older and weaker, your children began to speak to you as you once did to them.

"Lakshmi will help you bathe now," Srinivas said. "I will go and ready your bed for nap time after."

When Srinivas left, it was just me and Lakshmi in the bathroom. My knees felt limp and I started to fall, but Lakshmi pulled me up and held on to me. "Let me help you get your sari off," she said, tugging at the silk and twisting my body out of it. I felt guilty that she had to move her hands for me, so I avoided looking at her. But when she started to rub the Himalaya soap onto my shoulders as I sat on the stool, I had to look at her. I found myself holding her hands, asking from where they had obtained their callouses.

"From knitting," Lakshmi said, smiling. "I'm going to knit something for you soon. Maybe a shawl."

I held on to her hands tighter. I stared at them, seeing the beginnings of wrinkles forming. "A shawl for me," I said, and she nodded.

Keshav's anger began to rise in the presence of my knitting because he saw the time I spent on my craft as time away from the family. I had to find ways to knit in secret. There was a quiet creek by our house called Arekere, where I would go in the morning. I'd tell Keshav before he went off to the school that I was going for my walk. I'd take a ball of yarn with me and keep it in my coat pocket or under my shirt. I sat by the creek many mornings and afternoons, knitting sweaters and shoes for Durga, the girl who remained forever in my mind. After Rajan's accident, Neha moved with Durga to her aunt's place up north, in the small village of Kausani. I could never give the items I made for Durga to her, so there was a greater freedom in the making, greater room for mistakes.

The memory of Durga I held was from the first time I met her, in what had been Rajan and Neha's home at the east end of Bangalore. We sat outside on their porch, and I drank the sweet coffee Neha had brought for me. My brother and I had lost closeness after the year of the pot incident, and yet anytime I saw him felt like a blessing. He sat on a rocking chair, cradling Durga, and when I finished drinking my coffee, he gave her to me to hold. I looked at her, and already, her eyes seemed afraid, as though she had seen the many illnesses of the world in her mother's belly. Small spit bubbles rose at the corners of her mouth, and she reached for my finger. When she held it, her eyes softened, seeming suddenly less afraid.

As I was thinking of Durga, I heard the wailing sound of a veena coming from the other side of the creek. I looked across and saw a woman with a round belly sitting on a rock, her bare feet gracing the water. She held her veena and plucked at the strings. Then she began strumming, and the sound shimmered across the water. When she played, she closed her eyes and leaned into the instrument like she was disappearing into it. She swayed so passionately as she played that the rich, pink fabric of her sari dipped into the water. I wanted to tell her, but it seemed unimportant as her music grew, enveloping the space of the creek. She played an unfamiliar tune, one with melancholic notes like the soft cry of a nightingale. When she had finished her song, the woman glimpsed me. She motioned with her hand for me to come over to her, and the invitation frightened me, but I still went.

When I sat next to her on the rock with my yarn, she said nothing, but smiled and began another song. The notes were higher in this one, flickering between the tenors of extreme elation and the depths of sadness, like an explosion of colors, disjointed and yet somehow cohering in the end.

"This is about my daughter," she finally spoke. "Anjali. She died in childbirth." She glanced up at me. "What is your name?"

"Mamatha," I said. "Yours?"

"Isha."

"I'm sorry about your daughter."

Isha placed her veena beside her on the rock and held on to the folds of fat in her stomach. She rubbed her stomach as though there were still a child there.

"What are you making?" she asked me, eyeing my red yarn. I held up the half sweater I'd knitted so far. "A sweater for my niece, who I don't see anymore."

We let our absences linger in the air, and neither of us asked more questions about them—not then, anyway, though we did in the days that followed. But we let that first morning simply seep quietly into the afternoon, sitting easily with one another and reveling in each other's artistry in a world that did not recognize us as artists. She played more of her songs, and I listened, and they started to feel to me like prayers, like whispers toward salvation. The ripples of the creek seemed to move more freely when she played, and my fingers did too, weaving through the yarn, stitching closer and closer to Durga, to that child full of potential.

Now Lakshmi had moved to washing my breasts and stomach. She poured more soap into the washbasin, and the bubbles rose like pregnant bodies. "Sorry," I said to her, for many things, though she took it to be about her having to wash me.

"Don't worry, Amma." As she leaned over my wrinkled body, I saw that the sleeves of her salwar were starting to get wet.

"How is your hip?" she asked. It was a question asked to me every day, and every day, the answer was the same.

"Hurts," I said.

"If it doesn't get better in another week, we'll have to go to Dr. Khan," she said. When the washcloth touched my breasts, I felt the weight of time on them. It had been over a decade since Keshav had touched them, had wanted to, and now they shriveled like the rest of me.

I visited Isha at the creek for three weeks until she moved away. She had talked elusively about her plans to move to a smaller city, which would be more comfortable and affordable for her since she lived alone and on government aid. One morning before walking to the creek, I received a letter, slipped under my door, from Neha in Kausani. A neighbor's son who worked with Tejas had been able to find her address, and I had started sending her letters. They were long and confessional, and each time I sent one, I felt ashamed for the outpouring of words. I felt guilty somehow for the death of my brother, that somehow I had interrupted what could have been a perfect life for him and Neha and Durga. When he was alive, I had called Rajan, asking for money. Before Keshav got his footing as an administrative assistant in the engineering department at IISC in Bangalore, we had struggled monetarily. I knew I was a burden every time I asked Rajan for anything. He had wanted to forget his attachment to me since the day he lied about the pot, but I hadn't let him. I thought he resented me for that, for being the leech in his life, and I thought he resented me still when he died, his body spliced apart under the wheels of the auto rickshaw.

Neha's singular letter back to me, sent four months after my first letter:

> *Stop writing me please. I am trying to forget and selfishly you want me to remember.*

I brought the letter with me to the creek and showed Isha, explaining my story.

"I thought I needed to apologize," I told her. "I don't know exactly for what."

"Sometimes words just run in circles," she said. "They are useless." I supposed that was why she had taken to song. "What do you remember of him, your brother?" she asked me.

I tried to picture his face. "He was spiteful," I said. "And rebellious. And he was witty. And as a child, he was clingy. He wouldn't leave me alone. But then he only left me alone."

She began to play the veena. The sound was unpleasant at first, but it grew into a melodious song, a tune that settled like water.

"And Neha? How do you remember her?" she asked, pausing her playing.

"Kind," I said. "Her eyes are very warm. The few times I spoke with her, she talked about classical piano. I think she wanted to play piano always."

The sound of Isha's veena became softer, each strum of her fingers turning delicate.

"And Durga?"

"She had a lot of worry in her face when I met her," I said. "But it also seemed that she could learn to be happy."

Isha's song grew in intensity, and she pulled the strings faster and faster, creating a sound like a thundering.

At the end of the song, Isha turned to me. "Now we can start to be free," she said. "I will wash the dirt off my clothes." She held on to the pink silk of her sari and twisted away from it, then threw it into the water. I looked around to make sure nobody could see us. I had never seen another woman's naked body, and I feared I stared at hers too long, the way her breasts curved over her knees when she threw the sari into the creek, the subtle arc of her spine, the shape of her made whole in the light.

"Will you wash the dirt off?" I felt myself shaking but began to peel off my salwar, first my top and then my pants. I threw them into the water and watched the bright colors sinking, the blood-red orange, the bruising blue. I covered my breasts with my hands, but as the sun started to warm up my body, slinking up my hips to my shoulders, I released them.

"You are—" Isha began.

"I know, I know." She could see it all—my pointy shoulders, my uneven, dark brown skin, the splotches of scars from years of trying to scrub the darkness away.

She stood across from me, the round of her belly full like the sun.

"Beautiful," she said.

Lakshmi had finished washing me and now was drying me with a towel. We were still in the bathroom, and she stood behind me as she curved the towel over my body. "Thank you," I told her.

In the mirror, we were framed together, in the same image, my face beside hers.

"Come," she said when she'd finished drying me.

"Wait." I pointed at the mirror. I wanted her to see what I saw. The miraculous existence of our selves next to each other, how much time it had taken for us to be together like this.

I thought about all the cruel things I'd said about Lakshmi, to her and behind her back, all the ways I'd tried to make her feel she did not belong in this family. On her twenty-second birthday, seven months after she married Srinivas, I ignored her, standing in the kitchen with Manju and Karthik, talking to them about how awkwardly she moved in the room, seeming not to know where to stand. On her wedding day, I went up to her and told her how fair and beautiful Manju was, wanting her to know that she would never be. When she came to Bangalore for Keshav's funeral, as I was crying and spiraling away from myself, I told her I didn't want her to be near me and yelled at her to leave the room. She did, and Srinivas said nothing to prevent her leaving.

"Come, Amma, you're tired," Lakshmi said. She held my hand, and I stared at our two hands, clasped together, her fingers tired from moving through yarn, and I wished then, urgently, that she would never stop knitting.

She walked me to my bed and eased me to sit on it, then lifted my legs to rest there too. She covered my body with a shawl. "Take rest," she said and began to walk away, but I reached out for her and pulled her back. My hip throbbed with pain when I reached so suddenly.

"What is it? Something wrong?" She knelt beside the bed and faced me. I looked at her, the soft curling of her eyelashes, the cascading of her hair onto her shoulders, her eyes aged but shining, and wondered why I had ever been so cruel.

"I'm sorry, Lakshmi," I said quietly, quietly enough that she might not have heard. I was still a coward.

"For what, Amma?"

"I'm sorry," I said again. *It was never your fault. The ugliness was in me.* I closed my eyes and felt warm tears falling onto my cheeks.

She didn't say anything but simply patted my back. I didn't know if she knew what I meant, but I couldn't find a way to say more.

It was never your fault. The words circled in my head. My eyes closed.

In that blackness, I heard a faint tune, one that Isha would've played, oscillating between moods. I plugged my ears because I couldn't bear to hear it for too long. I couldn't bear the sound of my own guilt. The tears kept falling harder and hotter.

When I opened my eyes, both Srinivas and Lakshmi stood over me, their faces contorted with concern.

"What happened, Amma?" I heard Srinivas ask, but my mouth could not move to answer. "Should we call Dr. Khan?"

They couldn't hear the tune; they couldn't hear what I ached to say. I stared past their bodies, out to the living room, where, sitting at the corner of the cot were two balls of yarn, one yellow and one red, awake and awaiting their unspooling.

THE HEALING QUOTIENT

I WENT TO A HEALING therapist once my contempt for my neighbors had gotten out of hand. Every morning, they had a routine. I stood half naked, watching them, while eggs sizzled on the pan. They drank their tea and kissed each other lovingly, lips wet and warm from the other's saliva. At first, watching them repulsed me, and then it made me feel warm, and that I felt warm irritated me.

It had been three months since my breakup. One morning last week, I threw a bottle of perfume at the window as they kissed, and it hit the glass so loudly that the couple turned and squinted their eyes at me in unison, and then I flipped them off, and they looked more puzzled and my window was cracked, and I decided that I needed to fast-track my healing.

So I went to a place called the Healing Quotient that the internet recommended. The woman I met with looked like she'd had a bad morning. Her glasses kept falling to the tip of her nose, and coffee stains littered her pink cardigan. She recommended an exercise to me. It had propelled forward the healing of many of her clients, she said. There was a theater off Broadway for people who were struggling to get over exes—and a special room for those whose exes had already found new partners.

"You'll be in the theater alone, and with the consent of your ex and their new lover—we'll handle the communication and paperwork—you will get a glimpse into their life. You'll watch it like a movie, and the challenge will be to not look away. To confront your fears and then move past them." She added, pushing up her glasses, "Oh, and the theater's right next to that Indian restaurant. Krishna something. You could get some dinner there afterward." She smiled knowingly. I wondered if she had added in this comment because I was Indian. I smiled performatively.

On Friday, I drove the eighteen minutes to the theater and walked into a dark room. Everything had been set up for me; signs pointed me along, and ushers stood wordlessly, smiling and nodding. I sat in one of the back rows. I was alone. The movie began like an eruption. My ex-boyfriend, Colin, and Lila, who I had not met, rested together on a hammock in their backyard. A month after our breakup, Colin had moved into a house with Lila in his hometown in Mississippi. He had started seeing her at the end of our relationship, he said, but I suspected it was earlier. "We share a background," he'd told me. "It's hard to explain. I'm sorry." An hour before, we were showering together, and he had lathered vanilla-scented soap over my shoulders, kissed them. On the hammock, they stared into each other's faces, strands of Lila's blonde-brown hair falling into his mouth. But what made my little heart thrash around in my chest was the book Colin was holding. *Autobiography of Red*. We had read it together, slowly, over two years, retracing pages, lines. I heard his wavering voice as he read a part toward the end about Geryon's photographs. She pushed one of her fingers into his mouth. I winced, closed my eyes, curled into myself. They started kissing, and he kissed her tenderly, in a way he hadn't kissed me in a while. Early into our relationship, he began to shove his tongue into my mouth carelessly. He kissed her slowly. I ran to the screen. I balled my hands into fists. I yelled.

"That's our book, you fucker!" I punched the screen, and my knuckles screamed in pain. "Hey, Lila, you're so old, I bet your fingers are all wrinkly and so is the rest of your body." But she kept looking at Colin, and he kept looking at her. They continued on in their private world. My nose touched the screen. "Hey!" I yelled, but the darkness curled around me, and the screen became sturdier, an untraversable partition, and they kept touching, and I could not touch them, and they could not hear me.

But I could hear myself. The whimpering beneath the silence. The animal who had been there, waiting for acknowledgment. I listened. I felt her fur. I held her.

BLOOD AND BONE

WHEN MY DEAD FATHER burst onto my iPhone screen, he looked afraid. He sat in his tall, white armchair, white walls behind him. His surroundings had not changed, but something on his face had. It was evening here in Burlington; we resided nine hours apart now. I could only call him once a day according to the rules set out by the overseers of the antechamber.

I'd kept up my evening FaceTime sessions with Dad every day for the past six years. I'd had longer to talk to him than most mourners did with their deceased. The antechamber was described by most major news organizations as the holding place for spirits not yet ready to depart to the other place. Usually, spirits hung around in the antechamber for a year or two, but for some reason, Dad needed more time to mend before moving on. In any case, I was grateful for the time. I'd started calling him as soon as his Wi-Fi was stable enough, a week after he passed away. The only problem with having had considerable time with Dad was that we both now anticipated the day when his spirit would be ready and he would start disappearing.

"There's something I have to tell you," he said, eyes wide and earnest. I held my breath, expecting that the time had arrived. "Something's changing . . . in my constitution. They gave me notice last night. This is my final week here. Which means, I think, I'm going to be getting younger every day. They said my final form is younger and to expect mild to moderate nausea every night with the shedding of years."

"Oh." I watched him push up his round glasses from the tip of his nose. I thought that if I didn't say anything more, he wouldn't say anything more and, somehow, his inevitable disappearance would not happen.

"I just wanted you to know. So you can prepare. I disappear on Friday." His eyes gleamed with the residue of tears. I could tell he was trying to hold back his sadness.

"I know you don't want to talk about it," he said, voice dipping an octave. "We don't have to. There's still time."

I said nothing and was ashamed of my wordlessness.

"Tell me about your day, then," he said. "What jobs did you do?"

I went through the day in my head but felt tired from reliving it. The days had started to feel like a song running over and over, losing force with each repetition. "I did a commission for a woman named Aruna. An abstract. To express her daughter's *inner soul*. A lot of blotches of pink and red on a canvas. Have to do a final draft later. Mostly it was bullshit."

"Did she pay well at least?"

"$150. Not too bad."

Dad looked down at the table and swerved in his chair. When he looked back up, he stared straight at the camera, and for a moment, I thought he was in my room, sitting on the chair across from me, nodding his head in his steady way.

"Parvati," he said, reaching his hand out in front, touching the glass screen on which my face presumably bloomed. "You seem a little tired, Mari. Are you sleeping enough?"

"There hasn't been much time," I said. "Between all the jobs." I closed my eyes and felt a soft burning sensation. My rent was $775 a month, and art commissions alone amassed little money, so five months before, I had signed up with a temp agency called PeopleReady. Through it, I'd found work as a college essay editor, in reception at the hospital, as a proofreader and illustrator at a sleep science magazine, and as a freelance illustrator. What I really wanted, though, was time to make art of my own, to paint the landscapes I imagined. But as I worked more, I found my imagination was shriveling, drying like an old plant.

"Remember to take rest." Dad leaned nearer to the screen. "I only have a few more days to tell you this, so you need to learn it for yourself. Prioritize yourself." I didn't know how to do this while also paying for rent and groceries. I looked at Dad, the sincerity in his eyes, and I promised him I'd try.

When we hung up, I listened to my roommate, Eliza, rustling around in her room. I could hear everything she did because our rooms shared a wall. Now she violently opened and closed cabinet doors. It was Thanksgiving week, and in two days, she would leave for vacation with her parents in The Hamptons. She still relied on her parents' money for everything, though both of us were a year out of college. She was a perfectly nice person and had never done anything bad to me, so I felt guilty sometimes for privately harboring a mild resentment toward her, for the ease with which she led her life.

After the quieting of her noises, I was left to the silence inside my own head. I lifted myself off the ground. A sharp pain flickered up my spine, causing my body to bend forward; my forehead came to rest on my bed. I stayed in this position for a few moments, thinking about how I still had to finish my final abstract painting for Aruna. She asked for it for Friday. I imagined not sending it in. I imagined her sitting with her MacBook on her terrace, waiting for my painting, her flat-ironed hair falling over her eyes. I thought of her disappointment, pictured her telling the rich mothers of her daughter's private school friends not to commission Parvati Murthy. I thought of my bank account, the $14,000 emptied out, the *ka-ching!* sound at the evaporation of each dollar. I thought of all my value, all the measure of my worth, falling away.

Work is what killed my father. More specifically, the psychological stress it caused, physicalized into pains that erupted all over his body. He was a software engineer, but he always wanted to be something else. He wanted to be free, unburdened from routine.

With my head still buried in my sheets, I thought of Dad years ago in the prayer room at home in Portland, head bowed into the carpet. He didn't know I was standing outside the door, peering in through the slit. I was thirteen years old, and he was mouthing a prayer ferociously, a prayer whose words I could not decipher. I wanted to know what he was praying for. He looked up at the statue of Ganesha and squinted at it as though God had wronged him. He yelled, "Rank seven? Seven? After all these years? That's all I'm worth? Seven?" I saw his profile, the purple shadows under his eyes, pockmarks littered across his cheeks.

I later learned that Dad had given a presentation to his boss at FlexTech that morning, making a case for promotion to a higher rank. That he stayed at rank seven meant that, without Mom's job at the Montessori school—she had been laid off a few months earlier due to budget cuts—he needed to pick up extra work. This was when he started mowing lawns and fixing computers at local community colleges, and this was when his body started to droop downward, as though he could barely hold himself up, when the inarticulable hurt in his brain emerged as a crescendoing hurt all over his body.

I didn't know what I would do without Dad. I wondered what his disappearance would do to my brain. I'd heard that the second disappearance hurt more for some people, particularly for grieving family members. When the deceased disappeared the final time into the other place, some mourners could not deal with their grief. I'd read headlines about second-time mourners jumping off bridges once they understood they couldn't talk to the deceased anymore. I'd seen stories about people who'd gotten so used to speaking with the deceased that, even after the deceased disappeared with finality, they convinced themselves they could still talk to them. I hoped none of these stories would be true for me.

The next day, Tuesday, I had to work reception at the Fletcher Allen Hospital. Usually, I didn't have much to do, so I listened to the *S-Town* mystery podcast, reveling in John's bewilderment with sundials and the passage of time. As I thought about how I still needed to work on my final painting for Aruna, a woman ran up to the desk. A red gash gleamed right above her wrist. She had fallen while trying to hang up a poster of Bob Dylan in her teenage son's room, she said. Somehow, I couldn't look away from the wound. I kept staring at it, the blood, thinking how strange it was that wounds allowed us to glimpse others' insides, if only briefly. Sandra at the desk next to me entered the woman's information instead.

On the drive home, I thought about how I needed to tell Dad of my realization during our call that night. I anticipated he'd nod his head and say something about how what is kept inside cannot be contained for long. I stopped thinking when the pain slithered from the bottom of my back to my collarbone. For a moment, I feared I'd have to pull over and throw up. I stayed in a static position with my head resting against the seat's cushion. The stillness dulled the pain enough that I could bear it when I returned to my apartment. I hurried past Eliza making pasta in the kitchen and went to my room. I slouched on the floor against my bed and clicked on Dad's symbol on my phone. The picture of him was from 2012, three years before he died, in a rare moment of respite from his pain. He stood against a pine tree at Hendricks Park in Eugene, where we went every weekend before his illness rendered him unable to walk.

When Dad emerged onto my phone screen, his face was a constellation of pixelated dots. As time passed, the image cleared, and I could see him, though he was still a bit blurry. He was sitting in his armchair in his office, but he had become visibly younger. The lines under his eyes had softened, and tufts of black hair had grown in place of his bald patches.

"It's happening so fast," he said. "They told me I'm forty-one today. I don't know how young I'll be on Friday, when I go." His voice cracked on those last three words. Supposedly, when the deceased finally departed to the other place, they became the age at which they could best thrive, the age at which, in life, they had not lived to the fullest.

I felt an ache inside me, watching Dad become younger and closer to leaving. I decided I would try and focus on something else.

"Today at the hospital," I started. But Dad was looking away, behind him, at the globe on the shelf. He twirled it with his finger. I kept speaking, hoping that speaking fast would prevent emotion from overwhelming me.

"There was this woman with a gash above her wrist, and it was bleeding so much, and somehow I froze, I couldn't do anything, like, I couldn't even type her information into the system, I was just staring at it, thinking about how weird it is that when someone's hurt, we get to see their insides, just for a moment."

Dad nodded, speaking with a strange calmness and cogency. "In the end, all we are is blood and bone." He had told me this before, in the hospital when he died.

"Yeah." For the rest of the conversation, he moved around restlessly, looking toward the shelf, then getting up and pacing back and forth. I felt I was already beginning to lose him. Tears poked behind my eyes, but I suppressed them. I smiled at him, my anxious father, moving from one corner of the room to the other, never standing still, unable to be held.

When I was fifteen, in my first year of high school, Dad's pains started intensifying. He had begun working as a contractor for Portland Community College and Willamette University, as well as a lawn mower for a few rich families in Sherwood. Dad never spoke much about his feelings, but he could not disguise his suffering when he writhed on the living room floor.

I had been taking an introductory art course that year in school, and we were having a showcase. I'd made a drawing in charcoal of the postman from Dad's favorite R. K. Narayan story. I wanted Dad to see it, to tell me if the postman's turban had the right shape, if his eyes possessed the correct curiosity. He'd been working all day, first at Willamette University, then on the Lopez family's lawn, and then in the late afternoon at his regular job at FlexTech, attending to customers' queries about the new Oracle software he had helped to install. We were going to leave for school at 5:30, but when I descended the stairs, I found Dad on the carpet in the living room, arms stretched out to his sides as though he were making a snow angel in the absence of snow.

"Dad," I said, walking onto the carpet. "It's time to go." I knelt down and tapped his shoulder. He stared at the ceiling, and his eyes looked so bare I was frightened. He wasn't blinking, but his eyes glinted. He pursed his lips as though he wanted to say something. Mom came downstairs to the kitchen and grabbed a glass for water. "Mom!" I yelled. "Dad can't move. He's not saying anything." She told him he needed to go to the ER.

"Mari, don't worry," he said to me, grabbing onto my leg. His hands were sweaty, and a few beads of sweat clung to my ankles. "I'm fine," he said.

"You're not fine," Mom said, trying to pull him up off the ground. "We need to go to the ER."

"They charge a crazy amount, even with insurance, and the deductible—" His words sounded strained. Mom had not successfully moved him from off the ground, so he continued to lie there, angel-like.

"We have to go now for her showcase," Mom said. "But we can't leave you here."

He waved his hand in the air and said forcefully, "You have to go. She's been working on this drawing so long. You must go. I won't forgive you if you don't." He looked at Mom, and after a while, she said, “I’ll drop her there and come right back.” She pulled me toward the door.

“Dad,” I said, turning to him, but he waved his hand in the air again and told me to go, and so I did.

After Mom left the showcase, I tried to explain my drawing to my classmate Alex’s parents. They told me it was “vivid” and “imaginative,” but none of their words mattered. I texted Mom to ask how Dad was, and she said she was pressing a heating pad to his back; he still refused to go to the doctor, saying the pain was not severe. I kept thinking of Dad on the ground, wondering how much his words belied the reality of his hurt. When I looked at the postman, his turban sagged and his eyes blurred into the background, and his lips, frozen in place, could not move to tell us of his pain.

I spent most of Wednesday working on an illustration on sleep apnea for a sleep science magazine. I woke up again with a pain in my back and a feeling of tenderness in my head. I pressed my fingers to my forehead, and each press awakened a pinch. I could still move around, but the hurt in my head and back became a gentle throbbing, a familiar rhythm.

I became tired as I illustrated a man in bed, mouth ajar, eyes half-closed. Eliza had left in the morning for The Hamptons. On the kitchen counter, I found a plate of lemon bars she’d baked. I didn’t think I’d eat them because I hadn’t felt very hungry all week.

That night on my call with Dad, I described the sleep apnea drawing but felt that he wasn’t really listening. He’d moved even further away. He had become younger—he said he was thirty-eight now—and the rapidity of his unaging startled me. I knew he was still my father, but he started to seem like someone closer to a peer. I wanted to ask him about the pain in my body, if it was genetic, something many people in our family line had suffered, but he was distracted, and I thought it was nothing too serious anyway, so I didn't say anything about it.

The silhouette of a mustache appeared on the crease above his top lip. I remembered from Mom and Dad's old wedding photos that he'd had a mustache when they got married. He kept touching it, astonished that it had just appeared on his face that morning. He rose from his armchair and pressed his palms to the walls with a youthful elation. "I feel lighter," he said and repeated it, pressing the blank walls at different points as though something magical would burst from them. "Dad, Dad—" I said, trying to get his attention, but he didn't hear me, so I stopped speaking and simply watched him in his reverie.

The call ended much earlier than usual, and the premature ending left me feeling restless. My back and head still hurt, but I needed to get outside and walk. I walked the four blocks to Springwood Park and sat on one of the empty picnic benches. On the benches all around me, people were staring at their phones, squinting at their screens. Nine years ago, the government had put out a notice that mourners could call the deceased in public parks, citing the positive impact of fresh air on mental health. I heard the conversation of the woman on the bench next to me and suspected she was speaking with her deceased in the antechamber. I could glimpse her screen, though blurrily. It seemed the man she spoke with inhabited a white-walled room much like Dad's. She recounted details of her day working at an antiques store and then started whispering, glimpsing me in her periphery. She covered her screen with her hand. I didn't understand why it was something to be ashamed of, conversing with the deceased. It had been happening for a decade now in public, and for centuries before that in private.

The year that Dad died, I was a junior in high school and thinking incessantly about the future. I was applying to colleges and thought mistakenly that where I went would determine who I was to become. Dad was still working three jobs, and the pain still lived in his body. He had only gone to the doctor once and was prescribed painkillers but didn't take them, claiming that the doctor was a con artist. He didn't trust pharmaceutical companies or really anyone in the outside world; what he believed in was family, though he kept the extent of his suffering from us.

One evening, his legs became so stiff that he couldn't drive, but he had to mow the Robinsons' lawn. I drove him there as he sat in the passenger seat. I asked him if he really wanted to go if he could barely move his legs, and he said that it would subside in some forty minutes; it always did. I turned to him every now and then. He struggled to stay awake, his head falling limply toward his lap. I ached for him to rest, but there was a gap between myself and him, and I couldn't tell him what to do.

When I went to pick him up, he was making small talk with Mr. and Mrs. Robinson. Mrs. Robinson nodded at him in a polite but disinterested way, and Mr. Robinson rested one of his hands in his shorts pocket, the other on his wife's shoulder. My dad contorted his body awkwardly, leaning his weight on one of his legs, perhaps to relieve pressure from the other, stiffer one. He saw me in the car and waved over to me to join them on the lawn. I didn't want to, but I went so as to not be rude.

I was surprised to find Dad talking about the Portland Trail Blazers. Dad spoke in a groomed accent and lied that he had followed the basketball team's trajectory since we moved to town twelve years ago. I could tell he was trying to sound more "American," more like people like the Robinsons. Even his laughter sounded calculated, timed, like the laugh tracks on a scripted television show.

As I drove back home, I looked over at him. "Why were you talking differently to them?" I asked.

"You don't understand yet," he said. "Sometimes acting is necessary."

He didn't say more until we arrived in the garage. When I parked the car, Dad was staring down at his phone. He'd received a message from his FlexTech boss saying that he needed to work Saturday and Sunday night for an important customer and that it was imperative he did so in order to keep his job.

"I hate this fucking job," he cursed at his phone. "But there's no other option. Too old to do anything else."

I wished to inherit his pain so he wouldn't have to hold all of it. "Saturday night is when I mow the Lopezes' lawn," he thought aloud. I felt it was important I stayed near him, though he wasn't addressing me. "So how will I—I guess I can—no, that won't work."

We sat there for so long that the lights turned off and the darkness folded in around us.

He kept staring at his phone, not cursing at it anymore, just looking in a kind of resigned disbelief. Then he turned to me and grabbed my wrist, grabbed it so hard I thought it would leave a mark. In his voice, all the contours of desperation and sadness and hope. "Promise me something, okay?"

I nodded because I wanted him to let go of my wrist. "Promise me you'll never be a slave to anyone—not to your boss, not your friend, not the person you marry."

"Okay," I said, not really knowing what he meant.

"Promise me you'll know yourself as more than your rank."

"I promise," I said, and he released me.

Thursday morning, I woke with a pounding headache and a desire to paint. I walked over to the canvas Mom had gifted me at my college graduation but then remembered all the tasks I had to complete in the day. I looked out the window to the streets below, where children played hopscotch and jumped rope.

I drove to the hospital and closed my eyes at every red light. My eyes burned when I shut them. At reception, nothing much happened, so I worked on another illustration for the sleep science magazine, this time about sleep paralysis. The woman I drew looked truly miserable. Halfway through my five-hour shift, I was overcome with an incredible urge to vomit, so I went to the bathroom and locked myself in a toilet stall. I stood over the toilet, waiting for something to come out. I leaned my head against the wall and felt a sharp, throbbing squirming through my stomach. I wanted the pain to stop, but it wasn't incapacitating me, so I thought I was just being weak.

Back in my room, I sat on the floor and called Dad. I had two more calls left with him before he would disappear, before the Wi-Fi would go bad, before I would be truly alone.

"I'm going to miss you, Mari," he said. He was thirty-five today, and his moustache had grown fully in place. He was less distracted, but his intense focus on my face made it harder to not cry. He asked me what I did at the hospital, and I told him I started another drawing for the magazine. I told him that at one point, I almost felt like throwing up.

"Are you sick?" he asked, raising his eyebrows.

"I don't know. It's nothing that bad. But waves of pain come sometimes, mostly in my head and back."

"That's how it started for me," he said, reaching toward the screen. "Please don't ignore it. Go to the doctor."

"I don't have insurance. I'm just a temporary worker."

"It doesn't matter. Mom has some money. She can help you if you need," he said. He spoke with the passion with which he had that day in the car.

"This article about sleep paralysis, the one I have to do a drawing for, all the commas are in the wrong places," I said, trying to change the subject. Dad frowned at me.

"Mari," he said. It was strange for someone only twelve years my senior now to call me his baby daughter. "Don't ignore it. It won't just go away."

"It doesn't just go away," Dad said to me in the hospital the night he died. He spoke about his pain. (I don't want to narrate all of it, mostly because it hurts to remember and also because we've all heard enough stories about the magical things people have said on their deathbeds. I won't tell you much, but I will tell you about the slivers of light like slender fish that moved through the room, though the curtains were closed, and I will tell you about how Mom sat crying silently on the chair in the corner, how I hadn't seen her cry for Dad all my life, and I'll tell you about how when he closed his eyes, Dad looked like a sleeping child, peaceful in a way he rarely was in life, and I'll tell you about the way he grabbed my hand and told me that all we are is blood and bone, and how his hand was sweaty and warm, and how he told me to create things for myself, to not let my art become someone else's, and that if I wasn't careful, the work would take it all away, and I didn't know what he meant by "it," but I think I'm starting to know now, and about how all he had ever wanted to be was a gardener, to propagate plants and watch them grow.)

On Friday, my final day with Dad, my alarm didn't wake me up. It went off at 7:30 a.m. as usual, but my body felt so heavy with fatigue that I didn't hear it. I flicked to the email tab on my phone and found a note from my supervisor at the hospital with the subject line "Coming in today?" I didn't click on the email. Right below that one was an email from Aruna, asking when I'd be able to submit my final draft of the abstract painting. Once I'd dressed, I walked to the park.

Many people sat alone on the grass, headphones in, staring at their phones or at nothing. Everyone looked boxed in by an invisible cage. I found a patch of grass and lay on my back, facing the sky. I closed my eyes and imagined what I'd paint if I could. It had been months, a year really, since I'd painted or drawn of my own accord, and now that it had been such a long time, I couldn't think of what I'd want to create. I thought about what Dad would've planted if he'd had the time. Apple trees, probably. When I was five, he'd planted a Fuji apple tree, but it bore no fruit. No one understood why he was so deeply wounded by the tree's barrenness. He saw it, I now thought, as a personal failure. He'd have planted lupines, like in the story *Miss Rumphius*, which he had read to me as a child.

I stayed like that on the grass, alternately opening and closing my eyes, until the evening cloaked the park in darkness. People left and people entered, and the evening mourners scattered themselves across the large expanse of grass. Once settled, they pulled out their phones and pressed their noses to their screens. I wondered how many of the mourners would be losing their deceased for the final time tonight. I held my phone over my face and tried to prepare to see Dad. I didn't know how to tell him goodbye. I hadn't known how to say it the first time.

When he came onto the screen, he looked thinner, eyes brighter but sad.

"How old are you today?" I asked. I felt the wind moving over my face.

"Thirty-two," he said. "The age I was when I accepted an offer from FlexTech."

"So this is how old they want you to be. For you to live it again. Better." I felt a tightness in my throat.

"I do not take it for granted," he said and looked down. "These years of getting to talk to you."

The tightness in my throat intensified. I couldn't speak because if I did, I knew I would start to cry.

"Here, let me show you," he said, standing up and pulling three packets of seeds from the shelf behind him. "They gave me these today," he said. "Wherever I'm going, I'll be able to plant daffodils and magnolias."

I still couldn't speak. He smiled, but I knew he could see I was struggling.

"Where are you?" he asked. "Looks to be somewhere outside."

"Yeah. At a park. There's just no one else," I whispered, "who understands."

"Parvati," he said. "Look around you. People everywhere. Everybody knows something about loss."

I watched the man in a gray cardigan to my left, hunched over his phone, tears cascading down onto the plastic surface, then the woman on my right, her lips quivering as she peered at her screen.

Dad looked away, speaking to someone else. "They're saying I have two minutes," he said. "That I have to bring my flower seeds and then I have to meet them on the platform and go."

"Already?"

"I'm sorry. I didn't know it would be so fast. I don't want to leave."

"It's what's meant for you," I said, and then—I knew I was being selfish, but I couldn't control the words—"I don't want you to go. I don't want to talk to anybody else."

He darted his eyes around, and I could see that he was scared. I wanted to hold his hand, to tell him everything would be okay, but I didn't know that. I didn't know where he was going.

"I know it's hard. But you have to try," he said. "You have to give people a chance." We stared at each other for a few more moments until Dad dissipated, becoming a constellation of dots.

When he disappeared, I walked to an empty bench, cradling my phone in my hands like a baby. When I sat, I felt a jolt in my lower back. On the bench, the tears came, wet and warm in the creases under my eyes.

I remembered the moment when Dad accepted his job at FlexTech. I was seven years old and jumping on the small trampoline in our backyard, which I'd obtained after repeated pleading. He sat on the bench, slabs of wood peeling off.

Mom brought a sketch pad to the bench. "I'll teach you to draw, come," she said to me, and I squeezed myself between my parents, feeling unequivocally safe. She started the arc of a face, and I watched her shade in the eyes, the nose, the lips. She gave the paper and pencil to me, and I started to draw the profile of Dad's face. He smiled, and I drew curves to represent the creases around his lips. I asked him to turn toward me so I could see him better. He opened his mouth wide and stuck out his tongue, and I started to laugh, telling him to be still. Then he froze his face, made himself so unnaturally still that I laughed again. Mom guided me through the drawing, demonstrating on another sheet how to make the different parts of a face. As I drew Dad's nose, he received a call. He walked onto the grass and nodded his head, repeating, "yes, yes, yes," breaking into a smile. "I got the job," he exclaimed. "At FlexTech. Software engineer. Rank seven! In a few years, I could move up in the ranks. We'd be able to live in comfort here easily." Mom hugged him, and I looked down at my half drawing of his face, the lone irises of his eyes, his dimpled cheeks.

If he hadn't taken the job or hadn't gotten it, how would his life, and ours, have changed? Would his life not have ended prematurely? Perhaps whatever job Dad would've taken would've led to a similar outcome. The problem, I now began to understand, wasn't the work itself but what it revealed—his inability to articulate his own suffering.

I held my head in my hands. Dad would soon be in the other place, planting magnolias and watching them grow. He would tend to them carefully like children, keeping them alive. His tomorrow and the days after and after and after would be filled with growth, while I didn't know how I would proceed with my tomorrows.

An older woman came and sat next to me. Her eyes glistened too.

"You lost someone tonight?" she asked. I nodded.

"Me too," she said. "My daughter. I've been able to call her for three years. Don't know what to do now."

"I'm sorry," I said. "I feel the same way with my dad."

"How long have you been talking to him?"

"Six years."

"Wow." She twirled one of her gray braids.

I noticed I'd started crying again.

"It may be a long while before I feel better," she said. "Or before you do. But it helps sometimes to tell someone you're in pain."

I nodded at her and touched my phone. I clicked on Mom's name. I hadn't texted her in eight days. The last message from her last Thursday: "Wish u could come home for Thanksgiving. U sure u can't ?" I hovered my thumb over the letter pad, thinking what I might say. I wanted to tell her that the past six years, I hadn't really felt like I'd been living in the world, that I wanted to go home but no longer knew where or what it was.

My phone quivered in my hand. I turned to the woman, and she was staring at a picture on her phone—I guessed of her daughter. I stood up and looked all around me, at the grass, at the benches, at people crying and laughing and breathing and twirling. They moved and stayed still, buoyed by their idiosyncrasies, their fears and their longings.

I stood staring at the sky as it gleamed pink. I exhaled and breathed it in, the world, which glowed like a Polaroid breaking into color, like a statue coming slowly, imperfectly, to life.

HARSHAL

HARSHAL, THE FORGOTTEN daughter of Ajji's youngest sister, died at twenty. Legend says her boyfriend hung her because she did not want to marry him. I imagine her like this:

She walks through the market on Kalidasa Road, smelling the fresh chilis, the spice floating into her nostrils. She asks a vendor about the price of bitter gourd, then keeps walking, taking in the luster of mangoes and dates and okra, twirling in the summer light. Dust gathers beneath her feet, onto her sandals; the feeling reminds her of days spent in the sandbox as a child at her parents' first apartment in Bangalore. Her toes swimming in the pleasant, layered cold. The exquisite aloneness. In the sandbox, she birthed monsters and angels, gave them names. Back in her kitchen, she fills a teapot with water and places it on the stove. She drops cardamom and clove in the translucent pool. The water shimmers. She grates the ginger, cuts her finger, wraps it in a napkin. The blood gleams, spills out, evidence of her being. She stands at the window and peers down at the city throbbing between lives, and auto rickshaws beep, pushing past cows and throngs of people, and she wants to know where they're all going, and she pretends she does. Her mother hasn't come back from work yet; her mother hasn't weighted the room down with her sadness, so for now Harshal dreams. She watches a man carrying a handful of dates into an auto rickshaw and pretends he's her father, older now, an actor in absurdist local plays on the weekends. For today's show, he's playing a grumpy market vendor. She laughs at the ridiculousness of her story and peels away from the window. She throws milk and honey into the teapot and glides in her socks across the hardwood floors. She twirls as she did long ago in that first apartment, spinning long and hard enough to make herself dizzy. Soon the teapot whistles, sounding a tune, a siren screaming, the sound of something so alive.

A PURE THING

THE COUPLE LIVES IN LOUISVILLE, where he works as a bookseller and she works as a marine biology researcher. She makes more than him, and he acknowledges this happily. His laptop sports a colorful #Feminist sticker and, right next to it, a #ReadBanned-Books sticker. He understands hashtags because he must; he is still working on his novel about psychedelic meditation and an ashram at the end of the world. He's heard that Twitter—or TikTok—is where to get noticed. Privately, he bemoans this, wants to return to a simpler age. He is thirty-eight, just past what he feels is trendy and young in the literary world, but externally, he applauds his younger friends who have succeeded. He is in bed with his fiancée, Beth, the woman he met just over a year ago on OkCupid. She tosses and turns, a habit of hers he finds annoying, but she is carrying his child.

It's a Saturday, and on weekend mornings, the two of them go to the farmers market to buy fresh produce and taste artisan cinnamon rolls made by two local Latinx chefs. As a couple, they like to support the work of immigrants and their children.

They look perfect together, which means they look like they *should* be together, their expressions nearly identical, her hair just a shade darker than his. They look almost like siblings. Of course, they understand it's great to be a couple where people are different, but the two of them prioritized sharing a background. It just made the most sense to start a family from sameness. They *make sense* together. They live a peaceful life, and at night, they make peaceful, quiet love, and he enters her slowly, making sure not to hurt her, making sure to kiss her ever-expanding stomach where the two of them have made something, where someone resides who promises to be brought into this world.

Alone in her New Haven apartment, Ramya puts together a found poem. It's an activity of hers on Saturdays when she feels drained, and she often feels drained these days, in these after-college years. She needs connection but not from people. Found poems are about connection. They're about taking what doesn't naturally come together and bringing it together. She thinks often about the words he said to her. The words about his and Beth's shared background. She had felt his wet curls on her chest in the shower. She liked his smell, which was like soup. Campbell's chicken soup, even though he was vegetarian. He kissed her back, kissed her down to her butt, and he bit it, and she liked it.

Ramya met Isaac in a graduate literature program located in the mountains of a southern state. She entered the master's program directly after she graduated from college in a fog of panic, and she dropped out of it after a semester. It was because of him, but she told herself it was because it was impractical and wasn't leading her anywhere except toward unnecessary student loans.

She liked him because he was often alone and didn't seem to mind. He had been seeing Beth when they met, but they were open, and so Ramya slivered into his life, believing she had a place there.

It was simple when they spent time together at first—they took walks on the greenway, and he knew about birds, about their calls, and she liked learning about them. They stood by the river and kissed, and Ramya felt like someone would see and they'd be found out, even though they weren't doing anything wrong.

They ate tomatoes and olive oil on toast and talked about the books they were reading, the detective novel their professor saw too many societal implications in, the endings of stories that landed on images that were difficult to interpret. In his bed, she swam in his shirts, in the smell of his sweat as he pressed himself into her, the fur of his cats sometimes getting into her mouth. He licked her everywhere like he wanted all of her. This was why she kept coming back to his bed. She wanted to be wanted everywhere.

Later, when he told her he wanted to be with Beth exclusively, that they were going to start a family, she felt pins all over her body.

This isn't the point, she thinks, as she works on the found poem. He isn't the point. She presses her feet into the carpet in the basement apartment. She thought the apartment would be temporary until she could find a better place, but her new job with the art professor isn't paying her enough to find anywhere nicer. She refocuses. The point is the words. Why did it take her so long to get over this man? Her mother asks her this on phone calls. *This is your problem*, she says. *You get stuck somewhere and you miss what's happening all around you.*

The words. The time he told her, a few weeks before deciding to be with Beth, that they both knew he never intended to be serious with her. He said it flippantly, like it was obvious, and how could she assume anything else? How could she assume there were real feelings between them? He'd been messy with her, as though he wanted to get out all his messiness before he became a father. As though to be a father were a flip of a switch, something mature people decided to do mechanically. And the words he said to her once, at a local brewery, the two of them kissing before he said them: *I can be rougher with you; she can't take much.*

He could choke her and bite her and slap her, but he'd never do those things with Beth, who, he seemed to say, was softer, more serious, and then what was she? She couldn't stop wondering in the days after they separated what it was about her, her body, that made her so discardable.

He said she was beautiful. He said it many times to her, when she was on top of him, her hair covering his face. He loved her hair, he said. He loved her body, how he could bite her thighs. He did things with her he'd never done before with anyone. It made her feel special, and then she hated herself for feeling special. She sometimes thought about the other woman, and she searched her name on the internet, found pictures of her from various labs she'd worked at. She looked so simple, plain, her body the exact opposite of Ramya's. She imagined him inside of her, and when Beth became pregnant (a fact she learned from Isaac's Facebook page, even though she'd unfriended him), she imagined him cradling Beth's pregnant body and kissing her stomach, saying he loved her.

It's that I love her, he texted to Ramya later. She kept trying to block him, but she kept wanting to hear from him, for him to say something to her that would make her feel special again. He'd barely talked about Beth until he decided he wanted to start a family with her, and then he loved her, and he made sure to say this word over and over to Ramya, to underline that it was Beth that he loved, not her.

There was one time, before it all ended, when he'd convinced her to have a threesome with Beth. She found out later, calculating the timeline, that Beth had been pregnant then. Beth wore a dark brown dress, something plainer than Ramya would've ever worn, and watched Ramya out of the corner of her eye. Ramya wanted her plainness. She wanted to be clean like her. Her hair was short and brown and pinned back. Even in the throes of intimacy, it stayed intact, while Ramya's hair expanded, becoming more and more unruly. *You dirty girl*, he said to her when they were together, alone. Then, she liked being dirty, but now, all she wanted was to be a pure thing. Isaac's cats circled them, and Ramya watched them as Isaac gently licked Beth's nipples. One cat curled up beside Ramya, and she felt its fur, then it ran away.

Ramya kissed Beth, and her lips tasted antiseptic. She wrapped Beth's legs around her. She wanted to be enveloped by her.

He hid his face in Ramya's thighs, and he kissed her everywhere, but he did not say she was beautiful. This was the last time he touched her, and Beth was watching, touching herself quietly. As he kissed her, Ramya watched Beth, who sat at the edge of the bed, her finger pressed to her lips. Ramya made sounds and he kept licking her, but Ramya didn't look at him. She looked at Beth, sitting on the outside of them, though Ramya knew she was the outsider.

She arranged the words she'd cut out from magazines and newspapers on the floor. *The world's footprint*, *a sea of whales*, *the luck of clovers*. She didn't know what to do with them, what she could make. Ajji called her. Her mother's mom, the grandmother who lived in Mysore. She had been calling her a lot recently, perhaps because she knew Ramya was all alone on the other side of the country, or perhaps because Ramya's parents had talked about moving back to India. Ramya answered, and Ajji's face rose blurrily on the screen. She was sitting in the kitchen. Spices were arranged messily on the table behind her, exactly the way she remembered from the last time she was in India.

"Have you eaten, Rajkumari?" Ajji asked Ramya. In Kannada, she told Ramya she would eat soon, and then Thatha would give her an insulin shot.

Ajji's thoughts spun outward. She said Thatha was showering; these days, he took long showers. Before, he would be quicker, wanting to sit with her in the living room. Ramya had no memories of the days when her grandparents wanted to be around each other.

"Take care of your health," Ajji said to Ramya. "You look frail. Are you eating and sleeping properly?" Ramya nodded.

"Of course, and you take care of yours." But when she hung up the phone and went to the bathroom, she looked at herself in the mirror. She had become thinner, her stomach sunken in, her cheeks papery. She pursed her lips. It was these lips, thick, that he had bitten, sucked, until they bled. It was her thickness, everywhere, that he'd said he loved, and yet in the aftermath of it all, she wished to be smaller.

Some nights, when she left Isaac's apartment, she felt demeaned. It wasn't his words or the way he touched her that felt sharpest in her stomach. It was what her parents might have said had they known how he treated her. Had they known she'd been on her knees in front of him, even after he told her about Beth, begging him for a shred of his affection. *Why do you lower yourself this way*? Ramya's mom would've said, and the fault would've been Ramya's. Her fault for letting herself get hurt. Her fault for involving herself with a man who was older than her, in a different stage of life. Her fault for wanting. For imagining him as a young boy at the local theater with his father. For remembering.

When she left Isaac's place for the last time, the voices of her family circled in her head. *How could you be so weak? How could you be so boy-obsessed, so stupid?* She wiped the mascara off her cheeks. She emailed Dr. Hema Saraswath, a South Asian art history professor at Yale, and introduced herself as the daughter of one of her sister's friends. Hema's sister lived in Blossom Grove, a couple neighborhoods away from Ramya's family, and once upon a time, Layla Saraswath invited Ramya's family to her house with all the other Indian families in town. When she learned of Ramya's father losing his job, she stopped inviting them over. But all of that didn't matter. Ramya needed to use any in she could get to get away from Isaac, from the program, from the southern town in the mountains.

It worked. Hema was hiring for an assistant, and she must have been lazy or tired because she went with Ramya. Ramya dropped out of her program and drove the eight hours to New Haven to this basement apartment she found on Facebook.

Isaac left the program too, to pursue his plan of starting a family with Beth. His phone contact used to be accompanied by a photo Ramya had taken on campus outside the meditation chapel.

Now, on her phone, he was nothing, just a string of numbers.

Ramya's mother called her the last night she was with Isaac. It was after he said he didn't want her anymore, and yet he'd pushed her onto the floor and put himself in her mouth, holding her head and maneuvering it like it was an object.

It wasn't seeing herself as an object from his eyes that hurt her, but the sound of her mother's voice when she walked back to her apartment in the dark, how she couldn't tell her what had happened, how she would never understand, how she'd be shocked and disappointed and wanting Ramya to move back home and be safe in the family's embrace.

Was her family safety or the thing she'd run away from? She didn't know anymore.

What hurt her was not falling on the cold, uneven pavement, or the blood that gushed from her knee, but her mother's voice, asking her, *Putta, are you alright, are you in bed*?

It was thinking of all the things her parents had wanted to protect her from. All the disappointments Ramya had suffered and could not tell.

The remnants of the weed she had smoked that night lingered in her throat, and the night contorted in front of her into a monsterlike shape.

After he had released himself in her mouth, and after he told her to leave, her heart started pounding fast, and she thought she couldn't breathe. She told him she was having a panic attack and he stared at her, and his eyes were filled with the coldness of someone who did not care.

The person on the other end of the line, her mother, cared, and yet Ramya could not speak. *I'm okay, Mom. Yes, I'm in bed.* If only she could see how the blood dripped down her knee. *I'm okay. I love you too. Good night.*

One of the first things she did when she arrived in New Haven was go to the beach. The sand was soft, and she could bury her feet underneath it.

She rested on the sand, listening to Ajji's old voice messages. Ajji sent Ramya fragments of stories, asking her to record it all down.

Ramya listened to her voice. "When I was twelve, I found a book in my mother's bookcase." A sound like rustling papers animated the pauses between her words. "It was her journal. She wrote all the things she couldn't tell my father. My father was often away. She wrote about the smells of her body, how much she peed after she had all those children, the aches in her joints. But also her happiness. She used to play the veena beautifully. I played the veena for your thatha. He would sit next to me, and I played all the songs I knew. He said my songs were like the voices of birds. I taught him how to play. I don't know when we stopped sitting together. Maybe everything turns bad once you're with someone for so many years. We are like siblings now, not lovers."

Ramya opened her mother's voice message from that morning. "I know this must be hard, Putta. But you're following what you want. Don't feel any shame." When she told her parents she was dropping out of the program, she expected their disappointment, but they weren't disappointed. On the Skype call, they nodded their heads, told her the mountains were stifling her, that she should drive north, go to New Haven, get a new start.

Her mother's voice seemed to contain the same rhythms, the same pauses, as Ajji's. She spoke a combination of Kannada and English. Her admission wasn't a sad one but of a desire once had and released. "When I was younger, in Delhi, I listened to 'Take Me Home, Country Roads' and imagined what America would be like—roads and roads and roads that went on and on. I thought I'd learn to drive and I'd go through all the roads, the rows of cornfields, the mountains, the snow, everything. I thought I'd keep going until I reached something. We got in an accident going to Montana, and now I'm scared. I don't want you to be."

The ocean water circled around itself. She noticed the creatures beside her on the sand. With her fingernail, she felt the outside of a mollusk. It was cold and shiny. Her mom's voice moved with the water. "Being scared doesn't mean you should stay."

She held the mollusk, a clot of reddish-brown. The waves left and came back. She thought of her mother on her first plane ride to America, wondering about everything her parents had never told her. She thought of her ajji as a child, packing and unpacking her belongings every time she moved. Every time, another wound, another yanking away. She thought of her ajji's two braids, her unsmiling face, and glistening eyes. The waves grew louder. They touched her feet, and she left the mollusk to the water's embrace. The mollusk disappeared, gone when the waves calmed into silence. But beside her was the small crater of its absence, the impact.

THE PRETEND GAME

IT'S TIME TO PLAY, Soniya reminds her half-asleep brother, poking his shoulder. *It's almost morning.* The train comes to a jerky halt, stealing Arjun away from his peaceful slumber. He moves cautiously, like a statue coming back to life, his eyes blank, residing somewhere in the space between unconsciousness and consciousness.

What? I want to keep sleeping. He rolls over on his side on his makeshift bed, the red-cushioned seat he's been occupying for the past seven hours. Soniya turns too, facing his long neck. Even like this, she thinks, when she can make out only the profile of his face, he looks so old, so wise. She endures two minutes of silence before she taps his shoulder again.

What? He turns to her, irritated now. He looks down at her, the bridge of his nose the slant of a waterfall. She peers up at him as though he holds answers to questions she can't know. He seems to know so much, for he's nine years older and now a college graduate. Since he went away to college, he's been more distant from her and from the whole family. He got a girlfriend, and they maybe broke up recently, but he doesn't say anything about this. He hides a lot from her now. They used to say everything to each other.

Soniya tries to think of a distraction, one that will ease her brother into the game unknowingly. She glimpses the blue edge of the half-full Masala Masti chips packet peeking out of Arjun's seat pocket. This could be the diversion she needs.

Don't you want to finish them? she asks.

Not really.

Can I?

Fine.

She yanks the packet out from the pocket and brings it to her lap. She pulls the flap open, reaching her hand into the sea of chips and swirling it around aggressively for effect.

Could you do that any louder?

Sorry. Her apology is an impulse, but it goes deeper than the moment; it's also a yielding, a private admission that she knows she's a nuisance to her brother. She just wishes he would be less stoic, that he could be as excited about the pretend game as her. Without playing, Soniya can't imagine getting through the next eight hours of the train ride to Mantralayam.

Why are we going anyway? she asks her brother. He'll have some well-reasoned, philosophical answer, she knows.

But he just sits in silence and stares out at the dusty light, the faint outlines of pink and yellow industrial buildings forming the shape of morning.

I don't know, Soniya. He rarely says her name, only does so when he feels the weight of the world, its bleak and burdensome intensity. He says this quietly, nostalgically, like an old man sitting by the window, remembering the tapestry of his youth.

Don't you want to play?

I'm bored of the game.

But I have a really good scenario.

Mom and Dad are still sleeping.

But it's morning already!

It's barely morning. Some people like sleeping. Some people aren't owls.

It would be funner to be an owl.

More fun.

Whatever.

You're in junior high now, you should know.

I'm about to be in junior high, and I do know, I'm just not in class. I thought I was talking to my brother, not a teacher.

Well, fine, what's the situation?

She swirls around in her seat and props herself onto her knees, glancing at Mom and Dad, Mom's head hanging in midair, falling toward Dad's shoulders. Dad's hand rests on his thigh, his palm facing upward, as though waiting for Mom's hand. Like this, her parents seem closer, more intimate, than she's ever seen them before.

Woah, they look weird when they sleep. Like zombies.

What's your idea? His voice is growing impatient.

Okay, so there's this guy in north India—you can be the guy—and he wants to marry this girl, his childhood friend, who's, like, not as rich as his family, but his dad won't let him because of class differences, and it's a whole thing. I don't know who I'll play. Maybe the friend of the girl.

That's literally the plot of Kabhi Khushi Kabhie Gham.

It is? Wait, yeah, it kind of is. Oops.

You didn't have an idea! I'm going back to sleep.

No!

The last thing Soniya wants is for her brother to go back to sleep. If he goes back to sleep, then she's alone in this strange train with nothing to do but scrutinize the faces of the people in the seats in front of her. In the row across, alone by the window, she sees a man, tufts of gray hair poking out of his banyan. He reaches below his seat to retrieve a thermos of chai. He unscrews the lid and out comes a spiral of stream, billowing above his head. He blows at the chai, and the thermos shakes in his hand, his veins bursting out of skin, gnarly and arthritic.

I have an idea. She turns to her brother. He holds his chin with his thumb and pointer finger, as though at great pains merely to consider her thought. *Let's make up stories about the people on this train.*

Like how?

Like, let's start with this guy, the one over there, with the chai. Why do you think he wants to go to the temple?

To pray, probably.

Duh, I know, but—

Okay. Let me think. He's going to pray for his granddaughter in America. She's in her final year of a doctorate program in Missouri. Studying bioengineering. And she's getting sick. She's started falling down, fainting for no reason. She's got this gash in her thigh. And it keeps growing. She can't focus on her schoolwork anymore. She keeps calling her grandfather early in the morning; it's evening for him. Every night, he waits for her call, sitting by his muddy window. But her thoughts are getting confusing, more disjointed. She'll start to say something, then forget. He thinks his memory should've gone bad before hers. He wants to die before her. He's determined to die before her. It's the natural order of things. So he's going to Mantralayam for that, to pray for his granddaughter, for her health.

That was good. Sad. She feels a muted sorrow rising inside of her. She looks at the man again. He is eating now out of a tiffin carrier, hot parathas and okra palya and rice. He balances the steel carrier on his knees, and she listens to the rhythmic rattling each time the train tugs forward. *I can't do one as good as that.*

I'm sure you can, he says, patting the back of her head. He only does this when he feels a surge of love for her, which seems to happen rarely. She wonders what prompted it this time.

Aṇṇa, she says, *older brother.*

Taṅgi, he says back, playing along, *my younger sister.*

Ew, I hate that word. It doesn't sound as pretty.

Well, it's the word we have.

Maybe the people who created Kannada hate little sisters.

That makes sense. They're pretty annoying.

Soniya tries to think of what else to say. If she doesn't say something soon, she's afraid her brother will fall back into his still silence.

That lady's putting coconut oil into her braid. She's all the way over there, but I can smell it from here.

It's a scent that carries.

Why does she love coconut oil so much?

Hmm. Let me see. He closes his eyes, as though he's searching an encyclopedia of human stories in his brain. *Her older sister taught her how to braid her hair. She was kind of like a mother to her growing up. Their parents passed away when they were young. So to motivate her to get ready for school, the older sister would sing songs from that old Kajol movie—their favorite movie,* Bekhudi*—and rub oil into her hair. One morning, she braided her hair. And this woman, the younger sister, could smell the coconut oil in her hair on the bus all the way to school. The smell brought her a feeling of peace. So she still puts it in her hair now, to bring back that feeling.*

These stories are so sad.

Sorry. It's all I can think of.

It's okay.

Or, you know, maybe she just wants to force the overpowering smell onto us. Maybe she's evil. Maybe the oil will infiltrate our minds and steal all our thoughts, and she'll keep them and read them at the temple.

Yeah. I think that's what it is.

Yeah. Good we figured it out, he says.

Let's keep our thoughts safe.

Gotta lock them in a box.

We'll steal the man's tiffin and store them there.

Good plan.

She perceives the edge of a smile before it fades. He leans his head against the window, which she imagines is cold still; the light has only just touched the glass. The morning has only just risen.

God, how much longer until we're there? she asks. He glances down at his vintage analog watch, which he bought at a thrift store back home. Soniya knows her brother likes to feel as though he's living inside history, in the wrinkled pages of time.

Six hours.

Still?

Learn to go to sleep. It's what everyone else does.

But it's morning!

It's 6:48. It's the beginning of morning. And time loses importance on a fourteen-hour train ride.

He closes his eyes again, and Soniya is left to wrestle with her own self. She moves her hands in a circular motion, turning them over one another, picturing the gentle turning of laundry in the washer. She rises on her seat, propping herself up on her knees to take another look at her parents, who have moved slightly in their sleeping positions, Mom's eyes flickering half open, then closing, then flickering half open, like a buffering video. The train glides into the underground, and they are plunged back into the blackness of night. Arjun has either fallen asleep or he's just playing at stillness, but either way, he's stopped talking. Either way, he's somewhere else now, and Soniya is alone. She listens to his patterned breathing, like an AABB rhyme scheme, Dad's uneven snoring, and the sounds of the passengers, speaking and sighing and slurping, all of it melding into music. She feels the slithering snake of the train beneath her, hoping it will emerge soon into the light. She watches her brother, his serene face, his breath leaving tracks on the glass, and thinks how strangely at home he seems in the darkness.

LET ALL OUR GHOSTS DEPART

THE SUMMER AFTER I graduated high school, my mother and I took a trip to India. She wanted to show me all the sights I'd been lacking since I was a child: the Devaraja Market, where she would buy garlands for prayer decorations; the palace glowing at night; the small house with red walls where she grew up. We spent most of our two weeks in Mysore in her childhood home. I spent my days drinking the lukewarm coffee my thatha prepared and sitting beside my ajji, watching her knit baskets and shawls and listening to her spinning tales about my mother's childhood. The tales coalesced and diverged, winding around me.

One morning, early in our trip, Ajji awoke, believing that a ghost had possessed her. She insisted we go to the Sri Gayathri Devi temple, where the priests could perform a ritual to encourage the ghost's departure. It was bodily, my ajji's possession, shaking the core of her being. At night, when the ghost squirmed around inside her, she squirmed too, like an insect was swimming around in her depths. She began to sweat, and I went and sat beside her on the cot where she slept.

After a few days, Thatha and Mom gave up on trying to appease her; they left her alone to her wild, frightened dreams. I stayed with her during the nights. I asked if she wanted tea, water. "Nothing. I want to be left alone," she said, but then she grabbed my hand so hard she dug her fingernails into my skin.

"It's my sister," she told me in Kannada. "My sister moving in around me." Ajji was one of eight sisters, and now she was the only one alive. The last sister who had died, Geetha, had lived in the same apartment building as Ajji, on the second floor. Geetha was the only sister Ajji was close to. Up until her death, they'd drink Bournvita and play card games together, chattering late enough into the night that the neighbors had more than once told them to be quieter.

"She just has diarrhea," my mom said to Thatha. "Let's get her to the doctor; they'll give her medicine." But I knew it was something more. I stared at the gray circles underneath her eyes. She had given up eating most things and only ate balls of rice with ghee and salt. She said her stomach felt weak. She placed a hand on the round of it and guided my hand there. "She moves around," Ajji said. I wondered if Ajji thought she was somehow giving birth to her sister. I tried to understand the logic of this. Ajji had felt like she was the caretaker of all her sisters once her mother died, and her father, a geologist, was often away on work assignments.

"Do you see her still?" I asked, and she nodded. She gripped on to her nightgown, a faded red with yellow flowers. It smelled like dust and turmeric.

She told me she saw her in another form. She held on to her stomach and said, "She's splattered all over a canvas. Very blue." Ajji's Kannada was fast, words strung together. She started shaking and turned onto her side on the cot. The cot creaked. I placed my hand on her forehead and panicked. I thought that maybe I wasn't equipped to deal with Ajji's condition alone. I asked her if she was hungry, and she said to bring balls of rice with ghee.

I went into the kitchen, rummaged through the pots and pans, and found the mostly empty ghee container, which had some sort of black ink on the lid. I found the rice Thatha had cooked earlier and stuck it in the microwave. I hoped the sound would wake him or Mom. I put a few of the deconstructed balls onto a plate and brought them to Ajji. She ate from my hand, and it felt strange to feel a human tongue on my fingers.

"Better?" I asked. She stopped shaking when she was eating but then resumed her shaking after. I was still jet-lagged and couldn't sleep, so I decided to spend the night asking her about her sister.

I lay next to her on the bed. When the tremors left momentarily, she spoke. She covered my eyes with her hand, and it smelled of cardamom. I knew she chewed cardamom throughout the day. She whispered, and I imagined we were actors on the Kannada serial Ajji watched. In this episode, I thought, the granddaughter would magically exorcise her grandmother's ghost with the tool of love.

She told me about her sister. Geetha had only studied until secondary school, though she wanted to become a geologist like their father. As kids, she and Ajji would find red rocks in their yard. Geetha used the rocks to draw pictures on paper. Sometimes she rubbed them on her cheeks to make her cheeks look like they were blushing. Though Geetha was younger than Ajji, Ajji said she had a power over her like an older sister. When Geetha rubbed the rocks on Ajji's cheeks, her skin ruptured and bled. Geetha became obsessed with makeup. She stole into their mother's room and took her darkest red lipstick, smearing it all over her lips. She made herself look cartoonish. To be a cartoon, Geetha thought, was to be beautiful.

"Bring me that lipstick there," Ajji commanded in the middle of her story. I went to her dresser and touched her various items: the perfume that smelled like sandalwood, the gold-embroidered scarf, the thick red bangle. I found a single tube of lipstick, worn down. "Put it on me." The last time I saw Ajji not possessed, she was nearly silent, listening to Thatha tell stories about his time in the army, or with her eyes glued to her television shows. But with Geetha's spirit inside of her, words had been unleashed.

I followed her instructions. I'd never put makeup on anyone before, including myself. Maybe once. My hand was unsteady. I colored outside the lines of her lips. She told me to let it smear onto the edges of her mouth. When I finished, she was still as a painting. She smiled briefly, then lay back down. She closed her eyes, pursed her lips, and slept.

In the morning, Ajji threw up in the sink. Thatha yelled a bit, then cleaned it. Mom brought her ginger tea. Then Thatha got upset. He stood above her and asked her what had possessed her and told her that her sister had been gone now for four months. He told her she had to get on with her life, that this possession had stalled everyone else's lives. He used my name: "She's here for the first time in how many years? And she's here taking care of you."

He began a ceremony that he said would clear the ghost from her body. Mom and I watched, but I didn't want to. The look in my ajji's eyes—one of glassy acceptance—pained me.

She leaned forward in her chair so Thatha could pound on her back. He hit her with his fists, and she leaned into the bucket beneath her. "Everything will fall out this way," he said.

The next night, Ajji wanted me to put lipstick on her again. I did it because she said I was her favorite grandchild. "Like this," she directed me, wanting me to smear it all over her mouth. She described how often Geetha looked at herself in the mirror when she was a teenager.

I closed my eyes and imagined Geetha. The only time I met her as a child, she gave me Bournvita, and I drank it, the salty-sweet lumps of chocolate powder staying on my tongue.

"Stop looking at yourself," Ajji used to tell her sister. "It's not modest." But Geetha said it was powerful to stare at yourself, to take in all your beauty. "I want to see myself before others see me," Geetha said, applying another layer of lipstick to her thick lips. On special days, she put a layer of blue eyeshadow on her lids.

Many men saw her like that, covered in makeup, in what Geetha called her most perfect performance. Her full lips and long eyelashes made man after man from school, from the neighborhood, from the streets, come to her doorstep and offer her sweets and gifts for her affection. In secret, when their parents had gone out to the temple, she brought some of the men over and kissed them, let them fondle her breasts. Ajji could sometimes hear the sounds through the walls, and as she tried to study, the voices screamed louder until all that was in her head was the deafening sound of her sister's beauty.

She married one of these men, eventually, after leaving school. She had wanted to work, but he was a doctor and didn't think she needed to. He left her one day when he found a younger girl with rounder eyes. Geetha said she wasn't worried. She applied more eyeshadow, more eyeliner. There were more suitors at her door. She married someone else, but she couldn't have kids, so he left her. She told Ajji she would stay beautiful for herself. *Still, the men will look at me, and they will want me*, she said, her lips red and waiting. Ajji said she died when no one wanted her anymore.

Ajji slipped out of her maxi dress and kept talking, as though she didn't see me. I asked her if I should leave the room.

"It's nothing you're seeing," she said. "I'm mostly a ghost too." She looked through me. "Tell me, do you see anything?" She held her breasts in her hands, and I gasped. I didn't know what to do. They were brown and shriveled, resembling the dates priests would give us as offerings at the temple. She rolled herself into a gold silk sari from her closet.

"It's nighttime, Ajji," I said. "Get back into your maxi dress and let's go to sleep."

"There's milk in the kitchen," she said. "Go and wake Thatha, and he will make it warm for you." She sat on the bed, half wrapped in her sari, the top half of her still naked. None of it seemed scary, like nakedness sometimes seemed to me in movies. In the

Bollywood ones, there was hardly any nakedness; everyone was fully clothed but full of longing.

Ajji didn't seem full of longing. Her eyes closed shut, as though her nakedness made her sad.

I went to the living room where Thatha slept, his belly rising, a book of Hindu prayers on his stomach. He fell asleep with the prayers often, his fingers pressed together.

I tapped his belly, and he woke suddenly.

"Ajji's seeing things," I said. He groaned and went to the kitchen, prepared balls of rice and ghee. "Take these to her," he directed me. I felt the buttery rice between my fingers, rubbed the oil onto my lips. Ajji ate greedily, finishing the six rice balls on her plate in a few minutes. I watched everything like it was a spectacle.

In the morning, we women—Ajji, Mom, and I—went to the temple, where the priest performed a special ceremony for Ajji. My mom instructed me to bow down to the floor and pray. I didn't know what to pray for; my mind was blank. After a few minutes, I still couldn't think of anything for myself, but my mind wandered to Anish, the boy from Chennai who I had become friends with at my high school. He kept texting me, asking me things I couldn't answer, like if I was happy or sad. I knew he was bullied at school, and I wanted to be there for him, but I had graduated and felt unable to solve everything for him. I pushed him out of my head.

I watched the priest throw water into Ajji's face. I imagined him spitting on her. The water became wads of spit flying onto her skin. He threw the water so harshly I could hear it slapping her. When she came toward me, her face was covered in liquid, her kohl smudged over her cheeks. She wore a garland around her neck. She looked godly, like a flower queen. The white flowers hummed in the light.

She was quiet during the auto rickshaw ride back. She went to sleep shortly after we returned home. I watched her from between the curtains as she slept on her side peacefully, hands folded together to make a pillow under her head.

"She will be okay now," Thatha said, warming up milk with honey and cloves and placing it on her bedside table. There was something about Ajji being in this state of tremor that opened a warmth in Thatha, made him take care of her in a way I hadn't seen before. Whatever unleashed it, the tenderness sometimes slithered its way to my heart, and I found myself crying at night without even knowing why.

Mom and I hadn't talked much since we'd been in India. I think she was focused on her mother and father, their ailments, their growing older. Still, she spoke to me silently in actions, placing a blanket over my feet when I fell asleep on the cot in the living room, bringing me another idli when my plate had emptied. She patted my head at night when she went to the bathroom and saw me asleep next to Ajji. I had wanted her to notice that something was hurting inside me too, and tell me how to make it all not wrong.

Ajji looked renewed when she woke up from her nap. She stopped talking about her sister, and there was a spring to her step. She made her own food, preparing an eggplant palia. The oils and spices sizzled on the pan.

She brought me a plate of food, but I couldn't eat. I sat stoically, watching a commercial for toothpaste on the TV. "Why aren't you eating, Jaanmari?" Ajji asked. Her revival irritated me. Her cheeks flushed red, the blood rushing back in. It felt like a bruise was forming on my forehead. When I pressed it, my stomach felt nauseous.

Mom told me to go and rest. They would go for a walk in the park. She asked if she should buy any earrings for me, and I nodded absently.

I tried to make myself the balls of rice and ghee, but I couldn't figure out the rice cooker, so I took what rice was left at the bottom of it. The rice was sticky and hard, and globs of the ghee did not soften it. I ate it anyway and tried to fall asleep.

I looked at the text messages between me and Anish, the boy from school. I lay on Ajji's bed, smelled the scent of her on her scarf, the cloves and turmeric and lipstick. I rolled around in it.

Anish and I had taken a walk before I left for India. My attempts to ignore him were unsuccessful because he kept pestering me in many small, annoying ways. He left notes in my locker. I didn't even know when he got them in there—maybe when I turned the other way. In the hallways, he slipped by me like a ghost. That was the thing; to everyone else, he was already a ghost. They didn't see him, and I couldn't take being the only one who did.

We went to Eastlake Park. At the end of our walk, we sat down. I sat on a tire swing, while he sat on a bench. He resembled an older man in his proper stature, sitting upright. He asked me when I was leaving for the University of Pennsylvania, and I told him—the end of August. He asked if my parents were sad I was going so far away to the other end of the country. I don't know, I told him. They're happy it's a good school, I said. Where do you want to go? I asked. He said he didn't know, and then he said somewhere near because his parents were always worried about him, even when he went for a walk. Where do you go on walks, and what do you think about? I asked. He said he talked to himself, had conversations in his head. With whom? There were childhood friends. Adeep. Mayuri. People from school in Chennai. Where are they now? I don't know, he said. In my head. He wanted to talk to them, to call them up, but every time he tried, his parents berated him, said he should focus on his life here, now. That's why we left, they said. So you could have a new life. A new life. He repeated the words.

I wanted to text him, to tell him sorry. But anything I sent now would accrue significant expenses. I always wanted to tell him sorry, though I didn't know exactly what for.

I felt sick. I rose from Ajji's bed and went to the bathroom. I cupped my hands and waited for water from the leaky faucet to drip down. I threw some water on my face. I kept my eyes open and threw it onto my face again. I thought about Ajji in the temple, her eyes open, receiving the water from the priest. She looked like a fish, waiting for salvation.

Maybe I was just suffering from gas. Food poisoning. This is what some part of me believed, but another part thought I had inherited Ajji's sickness.

I went back to her bed and closed my eyes but didn't sleep. I heard rustling around when they returned from their walk. I wrapped myself in Ajji's scarf, and the evening disappeared and became night. I slept, and when I woke, it was still night. I smelled the air from outside coming in through the window. It was musky and full of flies. I opened my mouth, and one landed on my tongue. I spat it out and turned to find Ajji beside me.

Her arms were curled around her belly. Her eyes were closed peacefully, and from what I could see in her sleeping face, there was no fear. She even looked like she might be smiling. I unlocked myself from her scarf and put part of it on her. This way, Ajji and I would be together, safe from our ghosts.

My other ajji, Dad's mom, flew back with us to Oregon. The last time she came to our house, she spent most of her days on the couch watching TV. This time, she mostly spent them sleeping. All of us were on a strange sleeping schedule.

Since Mom and I came back from India, everyone seemed lost in their own undefinable stupor; even the wisteria on the balcony crept down listlessly, aching for rest.

Tonight, a Saturday, I felt restless. Since getting home, I'd been talking with Johnny, a boy who was in my senior AP US History class. He started the communication by responding to an old email chain about a group project we'd done together. "I remember you made this project actually fun. I had a good time working with you. What if we hung out for real sometime? You in town?" He sent it when I was in India.

The email was surprising for several reasons. Firstly, I didn't think he'd ever want to hang out with me, as no boy had ever initiated a social interaction with me. Secondly, he was in a somewhat popular crowd at school, mostly spending his time with sporty white boys, and I was not a sporty white boy. He had his complexities, though. Though history class was his only AP, he often aced the exams (which we all knew because our teacher called everyone up individually after a test or a quiz and told us—in a hushed tone but still audible to others—our grade).

The emailing began as a distraction. My mind was still spinning when I came home. I stared at my phone in the middle of the night.

When are you back? Anish had texted me. I told him I was back and asked if he wanted to catch up, but he hadn't replied for a week. I wondered if I should ask my parents to call his parents, but I never did. I just waited for him to reach out to me.

I'd been talking to Johnny all day. It was the first time I'd texted a boy other than Anish. The texting was boring content-wise, but I felt a thrill every time he said anything. Texting him was better than listening to Ajji snoring on the couch.

He said he was watching basketball and told me the teams that were playing. It would've made no difference to me if it were two entirely different teams. He told me he ate only Skittles and Starbursts for dinner, which made me wonder what his mouth tasted like. Then he texted me two words or, really, one word and one half word: *Ur pretty.* No one besides my mother had called me pretty before. The words made me feel something warm.

I felt my face with my fingers, the bridge of my nose, the flaking parts of my skin. I felt my throat and put my hands around my neck. Hesitantly, I slipped my hand under my dress, into my underwear. I felt around in there and then tasted myself. Salty.

I texted back: *Ur cute too.* The action felt stupid, and as soon as I sent the text, I wanted to unsend it, but almost immediately, he responded: *;).* Then, another green bubble: *Want to meet at Whale Park? Yes*, I responded quicker than I could interpret what I had said. He sent me the address, and it was a fifteen-minute drive from my house, farther than I'd ever driven alone. School was only five minutes away. But I'd committed, and I couldn't say no now.

I checked that everyone was asleep and tiptoed down the stairs. I knew the slyest way to leave the house without making much noise was to go to the backyard and exit through the gate.

Johnny was waiting in the parking lot in a silver Lexus. I didn't know much about cars, but I knew this was a nice one. I parked right next to him. There was no one else in the parking lot. Was this even a place where people walked? Johnny's face was blurry behind the glass. I stepped out of my parents' Corolla, and he motioned for me to come inside. I wondered where the park was, if we were going to take a walk. I asked him this when I sat in the passenger's seat. He laughed. I could see the hairiness of his arm. I focused on the patterns of his hair, where it was thick and thinner. I hadn't noticed in history class that he had so much hair on his arms.

He pressed his lips to my forehead. That he went for my forehead first seemed oddly tender, but then he bit my neck greedily. I pushed him away. "Do you remember how Mr. Kerner would always say his weekend was 'moderately enjoyable'? Why'd he always use that descriptor?" I asked.

He said nothing.

"Should we get some ice cream?" I asked.

His green eyes glimmered. "Stop being silly," he said. "I know what you want." What did I want?

I reached into my pocket for my phone. He was kissing my neck, and my arm was crushed by his weight.

"You ever been touched before?" he asked with a smile.

"Yes," I said. "A few times." I closed my eyes and imagined my lips were painted red, my eyes shadowed with blue. I saw my ajji standing in front of her mirror in Mysore, lips smeared with dark red lipstick. This is what beauty was, she said. This is what beauty made you into. The way she said it made beauty feel sinister: people looked at you but as an object on display.

That was the night she peeled off her maxi and showed me her breasts matter-of-factly. I remembered them, the drying prunes. I wanted so badly to be seen, to not fade away like Anish, who spoke meekly and bowed down his head. It was not long ago that I was Anish, eating alone in the cafeteria, hiding my oily paratha under a brown paper bag.

I felt something sharp inside of me. It was his finger. He pulled it out and looked at my face, searching for a reaction. I smiled because that was what I was supposed to do. He called me his doll and cupped my cheeks. "Am I beautiful?" I asked, feeling the hollowness of my question.

"A beautiful doll," he said. I felt like he was playing a part, and I was too. It was necessary as a woman to play a part, I understood. It was what Ajji had done when Thatha hit her back, pushing the ghost out of her. I saw in her eyes that she could fight back, but her passivity gave her protection. To be protected was to be cared for. It was what her sister had done to make men trace the contours of her lips, confessing their love to her.

I closed my eyes and saw my ajji, her helpless fish eyes in the temple. I saw us looking into a mirror, her face right behind mine, a version of mine.

I conversed with her in my mind. I told her I was sick and that a boy at school was sick and I didn't know what to do. "We have to take care of ourselves," she told me in Kannada, her hand on my shoulder. "You can't let someone else swallow you up. Then you'll disappear too."

I blinked hard, then bit my lip. "Bite my lip," I told Johnny, and he obeyed. I kissed his neck and smelled his cologne, intense and overpowering. I licked his skin and tasted whatever he sprayed all over himself. I felt his cold fingers prying me open.

It hurt, but I thought I would endure it and then it would get better. But it didn't, and his nails were sharp. I would endure it because I was finally desired by someone, and I was not Anish; I was someone to be looked at.

He dug his fingers in deeper. They burned. I asked him if we could get ice cream. I tried pushing his arm away, but he was much stronger than me. My desire turned quickly into fear. I thought of Ajji's eyes when Thatha pounded her back, trying to get the ghost out. I thought of Anish, wandering around the school parking lot, listening to the voices in his head. Any moment now, Thatha said, hitting her, the ghost would come out of her and she would be free.

He had two fingers in me, then three. I winced and let out a yelp. Why wasn't he stopping? "I want to get ice cream," I told him.

"You don't need ice cream," he said and squeezed the fat of my thighs before pushing three fingers back inside of me. I breathed in and out. I reached for my phone in my pocket, but I couldn't see if there were any messages. I couldn't do anything, and finally, I stopped squirming and let his fingers burn me. He put another finger in, and then his whole fist, and I imagined myself breaking, decomposing into particles of light.

When he was done, he pulled his fist out of me and started speaking. I couldn't hear him; it seemed he was just making motions with his mouth. Finally, he told me to leave his car, and he left. Another car drove slowly into the parking lot. I wished it was one of my parents with Ajji in the back seat, coming to rescue me. I imagined the warmth of my mother's hands on my hair, lathering coconut oil into it. I imagined warmth, but everything around me was cold. The car circled the parking lot, then drove away.

I decided to get ice cream on my own. I was the last customer in the Baskin-Robbins at the plaza. I got the cotton candy, my favorite. The whole drive there, the car seat felt full of pins. The flesh of my thighs was tender, the insides of me scratched out.

With my ice cream, I sat in the Corolla and watched the lights inside the Baskin-Robbins flicker on and off as the woman who had served me cleaned down the counters. She wiped them methodically. I concentrated on the motion as tears fell from my eyes.

Families and groups of friends passed by in front of me, talking and laughing. Their sounds moved into me, flowed out of me.

Ajji texted me on WhatsApp. She must have just woken up. *You are feeling better now?* I saw the missed calls and messages from my mom. *Where are u? You left the house and im worried.* I told her I'd just gone out to practice driving and listen to music. I knew she'd be upset, but the lie was enough to tide her over until I got back. *Everyone was asleep*, I added to my text. *I was bored.* I could see her texting back, but I didn't want to read her messages.

I put a finger inside myself and pulled it out, seeing my own blood. It looked strange, thick and pinkish. In India, Ajji looked afraid when the ghost of her sister thrashed around in her, but I didn't see her cry. I didn't see her bleed. But I knew how much she was hurting. I knew now that at the center of Geetha's performance was pain. I imagined Geetha's face, bare, growing older, the lines across her skin etchings of our shared history. I imagined her shutting the door on every suitor that came to her, cutting this disease from her life away. I heard her screams from the room next door, and she was saying a word: *No, no, no.* I listened.

The Baskin-Robbins was all dark now, but the world around it was still bright. It was a beautiful summer day. I let go of the cone, and the ice cream fell into my lap, onto my dress, its colorful mess splattering all over my thighs. It was beautiful, a mixture of blue and pink and yellow. A beautiful brightness, all over my skin.

ADALITA

THE SOUP HUMMED on the stove, and the teakettle screamed. Manoja watched her daughter Pooja flinch in pain as Abhi, Pooja's two-year-old son, beat at her leg. Pooja stood, a stoic statue accepting every hit, simply closing her eyes as her son hurled himself at her. Manoja imagined a wet and gaping gash forming beneath Pooja's green pant leg, and she could almost see the blood peering through the fabric. Some primal desire to protect her daughter activated; she lunged forward and yanked the child out of his mother's arms.

"What're you doing, Mama?" Pooja asked, eyes wide and bulging.

"I thought I was saving you."

"From my own son?"

"He was hurting you."

"He's *two*."

"But he was still hurting you."

"Just go and sit over there, Mama," Pooja said, waving her hand in the direction of the couch.

Manoja's daughter and grandson had come from San Francisco to visit her in her Oregon home for the weekend. Abhi had spent most of last evening and this afternoon blowing spit bubbles or screaming out incoherent fragments of words. Manoja feared that her daughter saw visiting her as another task she had to complete, something else to cross off her infinite to-do list. Being old and alone did this to you. The cruelty of time transformed you into a pitiable object, even in the eyes of the person to whom you gave life.

"No," she said defiantly as Abhi returned to Pooja's arms, calmly now, as though his outburst moments before had not occurred. His eyes, green and glimmering, stared out at Manoja, almost monstrous in their eerie beauty. Manoja looked at him and could not process that he shared any of her blood; he seemed so distinct from her, so clever and cunning at such a young age. He bit Pooja's wrist, his little teeth leaving an imprint that faded in seconds. And then another fit began: "Rejist-uh," he yelled, and again, more forcefully, "*Rejist-uh!*"

"Shoot, I didn't bring it here," Pooja said. "His toy cash register."

"Oh."

Her daughter and grandson's weekend visit had reminded Manoja of the trials of raising a child, how unbearable and annoying the process could be. (How rewarding too, of course, but this was beside the point.) The child's sharp screams pierced Manoja's ears, grating like chalk on a chalkboard, until she couldn't take the sounds anymore and asked, "How to make it stop?"

"He wants his toy."

"Well, you didn't bring it."

"Didn't I used to play with one of those? Might it be somewhere in the house, in one of those boxes in the garage?" Abhi had transitioned to alternately biting Pooja's pointer and middle fingers.

"I can go check." Manoja had no idea where she'd kept the cash register toy, but she took this opportunity for respite from Abhi's devilish behavior. She walked to the laundry room and put on her black loafers, then went to the garage, flicking on the light. The sight—the mess of boxes toppled over, old jackets and papers strewn about—horrified her, and yet she knew this chaos had erupted from within herself in the past two years after her husband had left the world. She sank deeper into the garage and opened the bottom drawer of the side cabinet, finding a stack of papers curling at the edges: a manuscript from her years working as a proofreader at Inscribe Press, a middle-grade romance and fantasy publisher. She flipped through the pages, remembering the improbable plot points of the story, wherein the heroine, Carissa, transformed into a butterfly princess at the touch of a torrent of lightning and subsequently fell in love with the forest king Calyx, a half-tree, half-man ruler of bark and leaves.

She glimpsed a box on the floor, fallen over and filled with stuffed toys once belonging to a young Pooja. Manoja lifted out two animals from the box: a gray rhinoceros, its mouth spread wide in a smile, and a round, pink manatee. Pooja had loved the manatee in particular, taking it with her everywhere, even on vacation to Munich, holding it close to her chest at the Marienplatz and the Nymphenburg Palace. At the bottom of the box, underneath a wide array of stuffed animals, lay a photo album, golden leaf patterns embedded into its auburn cover. Manoja took the album and brought it with her to the garage steps. She placed it on her lap and opened it, shocked by the sight of her twenty-seven-year-old self standing with Saurabh under the Hawthorne Bridge. They had married a month earlier, and their skin shone, translucent, their eyes giddy with joy, the shadows of the river and trees dancing across their taut faces. She smiled at the photo, entranced by Saurabh's thick, curling moustache and his bell-bottoms, almost forgetting the nights that followed, of screaming and throwing cutlery and pressing her hand over his lips, trying to block the sound of his yelling, his bubbling saliva gathering on her palm. Seeing him like this, so young, all his latent potential inside, she almost forgave him for his inscrutable insecurities, for leaving her alone in this house.

She kept turning the pages of the album, moving fast through time, past herself cradling newborn Pooja in the hospital, past Pooja's first trip down the yellow slide in the backyard, until she was halted by a black-and-white photo, covered in dust, falling out of its slot. It was of herself before she knew Saurabh. She sat inside a Marshall High School bus with Adalita, the Australian girl who had been her only friend in those years. She must have tossed the album here during that frenzied period of trying to sell the house after Saurabh died. Manoja's mother had taken the photo, waving them goodbye in the early, sickening hours of morning. In it, their noses touched the bus window, Manoja's cheek grazing against Adalita's. Along with the rest of the speech and debate team, they were on their way to Silverton for a tournament. The bus had started to move, jolting Adalita out of her morning drowsiness, prompting her to scrunch her nose and pull at one of her braids.

Pooja's voice came like a knife, severing the cord of memory. "Dinner's ready," she said, climbing down the three steps into the garage. "Did you find the toy?"

"I couldn't."

"Did you look in all the boxes?"

"A few. So many here."

"Here, let me look," she said, brushing past Manoja and rifling through the box of stuffed animals. Manoja closed the album but continued to grip the photo.

"It makes me so tired," Manoja said.

"What?"

"Seeing all the stuff."

"We've got to get more energy into you," Pooja said.

"I'm not a wind-up toy."

"I didn't say that. Just, you have so many more years."

"Maybe not."

"Don't be dramatic," chided Pooja.

"You never know."

"Now where could this thing be?" Pooja moved to the boxes in front of the Jeep, rummaging through Saurabh's old clothes.

"I don't know. I threw everything in here without thinking."

Pooja sighed and stuffed Saurabh's musty science-museum T-shirts back into the box. "Abhi's probably getting hungry. I'll look more later." Manoja heard Abhi's wailing inside, like a distant siren. "Maybe we'll find it tomorrow," Pooja said, walking to the door. "Should we go eat?"

"I'm not that hungry."

"You have to try and eat."

"I don't want soup. All I want is ghee."

"You can't just eat ghee. Not good for you."

"Wish it was."

"I know," Pooja said, ascending the steps and walking inside, the door clicking shut behind her. She hadn't noticed or asked about the album on Manoja's lap. As easily as Pooja had gone inside, Manoja felt she could disappear back into her plastic San Francisco life and job at the PR firm. Manoja wondered if submerging herself in shallowness was her daughter's coping mechanism for the constant little tragedies of living.

Before following Pooja inside, Manoja opened the album once more, drinking in the details of herself with Adalita, their faces staring out, small and sincere.

Pooja spooned the broccoli soup into Abhi's mouth, and he spit it up, leaving a trail of green mush on his white shirt. Manoja watched Pooja frantically rubbing at the textured stains and wiping at the corners of Abhi's mouth.

She wanted to ask her daughter if she was lonely with Noah gone so often for work, but she knew the question would be met with deflection, some vague response about her weekly hikes with other mothers, some of them single mothers, or Thursday happy hours with her coworkers. Pooja knew how to bury her discontentment under a shield of busyness, something, perhaps, that Manoja had inadvertently taught her.

The green liquid in Manoja's bowl clotted and congealed, becoming less appetizing with the passing of each second. Pooja had bought the prepackaged soup from Trader Joe's, along with a host of other frozen meals, to stock the fridge with "quick and easy nourishment" for Manoja after she left on Monday. Though she did not tell Pooja this, Manoja was grateful for her daughter's efforts, for she could barely make it out of the house anymore, a potent fatigue making a home for itself in her body. She thought often about moving away to some small apartment in a quiet part of the city, somewhere on the outskirts without hip bars or restaurants, where she could be left alone. She'd never summoned the energy to bring that wish to fruition.

Pooja vacantly eyed the table, not seeming to see the tablecloth or the wood. "Ma," Abhi yelled, pulling her out of her brief reverie. "Ma, ma, ma!," he continued, an unending chorus. "Shh, shh," Pooja calmed him, tearing off a piece of bread and placing it in his tiny mouth. A dusting of flour fell onto the blue tablecloth. Manoja stared at the tablecloth, the flour spots forming milky stars in a blue and faraway sky. Outside, the black night arrived.

Upstairs, in front of the long mirror in her room, Manoja peeled off her beige pants and black button-down shirt. She turned toward the bed, and its expansiveness suddenly alarmed her, as though all the space could enter her and deepen the void within. She went to her closet and retrieved her plain, dark blue maxi gown, one just like her mother used to wear, and she put it on and slid under the blankets in her bed. She had given up on brushing her teeth at night. There was no one to taste her breath anyway.

Pooja slid into the room and sat on the edge of Manoja's bed, the white fleece blanket crumpling under her.

"I just wanted to say good night." Pooja had not done this since she was a child, and Manoja wondered what had prompted such tenderness.

"Good night, Mama," Pooja said, stroking her mother's hair. She smiled, then lifted herself off the bed, turning toward the door, but Manoja grabbed hold of her arm so tight that Pooja turned back to her, exclaiming, "Ow! Stop!"

"Stay," Manoja said, releasing her grip.

"I have to check on Abhi. We need to sleep."

"But don't you want to know?" Manoja asked, feeling her heavy eyes. "About the pain?"

"I don't know what you're saying, Mama. Please get some sleep."

"I don't want to sleep anymore."

"Well, I do. I'll see you in the morning," she said, and she left.

She left Manoja alone. Manoja turned off the bedside lamp, residing once again within the dark walls of her mind. If she were Pooja, she thought, she wouldn't have wanted to be around herself either. She closed her eyes and remembered Pooja as a young girl, swaying on the red swing in the backyard. She wore a blue frock dress, one Manoja had picked out, and flashed her toothless smile at Manoja, her curly hair matted in the front. She clung on to Manoja's leg like a koala, refusing to let go, even when Manoja needed to go to work. To be needed like that. It had been a long time since Manoja had known this feeling.

She thought about the girl she had been in the school bus photo. She thought about the girl she was always with. Her friend Adalita seemed like she never needed anyone, though Manoja knew this wasn't true. Through all four years of high school, she'd never asked Manoja where her family was from, which, at that time, was rare and a relief. Their point of connection had been speech and debate, though they had joined the club for different reasons, Adalita being more of a debater and Manoja a performer of dramatic script and poetry. Sophomore year, when the photo was taken, Manoja was performing Sylvia Plath's bee poems, about which Adalita could spin out interpretations for hours. Manoja liked listening to her thoughts as her mind swung between absurdity and the intensely cerebral. Adalita's voice sounded to her like music. Manoja's favorite part of the weeks were the bus rides to the tournaments, for during those rides, Manoja could exist in the same frame with Adalita, watching the light fall on her shoulders as the bus pulsed forward, and time was a run-on sentence, not yet arrived.

During breaks at the tournaments, they would run to the bathroom and debrief on their rounds or gossip about the other schools' competitors' dry and predictable monologues. Once, Manoja went inside the stall with Adalita, standing with her back to the door as Adalita rolled down her tights and sat on the toilet to pee. Manoja stared at the curvature of her legs, the way her thighs almost touched but didn't, the sharpness of her collarbones as she leaned over to reach the toilet paper. Adalita didn't tell her to look away.

Boys were the only rupture to their time together. They were always falling over for Adalita. Adalita settled for a few, but she'd dump them in a week or two and tell Manoja stories of their stupidity and clumsy ineptitude: how they slobbered like dogs when they kissed, how they tried to impress her with cheesy and badly memorized Shakespeare sonnets. These stories were Manoja's favorite part of the cycle—when the boys became anecdotes in Adalita's mind.

That's how they were, inseparably linked, until they weren't, until they got older and left school and Adalita married a real estate agent and moved to Utretcht, and Manoja met Saurabh in a youth group at a Hindu temple during her first assignment as a reporter at *Portland Mercury*, and he touched her shoulder, and she flinched, first with surprise, then delight, and they gave themselves to each other and got married, and his engineering job consumed him and started to make him unhappy, and he lashed out at her and baby Pooja, and Manoja tried to protect her daughter by making her body into a blanket, growing layers of fat around her like walls, and she tried to call Adalita in the late mornings when Saurabh had left for the office and Pooja was napping, but the conversations waned, turned cursory, until they stopped entirely, and Saurabh stopped wanting her at night, looking past her at the TV, and the bottles of alcohol accumulated under their bed, and one night, he drank too much and became still, and he left her to this house alone, and Pooja grew up and left too, and Manoja was left floating, suspended inside a skeletal existence.

But before all this happened, before the transpiring of these events, it was the year 1983, and Manoja was eighteen, in her first year at Boston College, and she had gone to visit Adalita at Wellesley during her fall break. Adalita appeared disheveled when she received Manoja at the train station, clad in an oversized Wellesley debate sweatshirt and large hoop earrings, her eyes red and mascara scarring the craters below. By the time they ambled through the quad and made it back to Adalita's room, it was too late to go to the dining hall, so they just sat on Adalita's bed eating stale saltines, crumbs getting all over her sheets. Adalita's room smelled like weed; Manoja didn't remember her smoking in high school. She'd been shaken by a boy, the debate captain, who'd broken up with her that morning. He told her that she was "too in her head," and these words, not his breaking up with her, had bothered her, slithering their way under her skin.

"As though it's wrong to live inside one's head," Adalita scoffed.

"The mind is the best home," Manoja reassured her, lowering her back to the bed. Adalita lay down too and pulled her blanket over the two of them. They remained like this in silence until Adalita said, "We're reading Sylvia Plath in class. The bee poems."

"The bee poems!"

"I keep thinking about your performance. And 'Wintering.' The final line. 'The bees are flying. They taste the spring.'"

"It's a good line."

"What do you think it means?"

"I don't know, actually. I never really knew."

Adalita rested her chin on Manoja's shoulder and glided her hand across the smooth surface of Manoja's belly, slipping her finger in and out of her belly button, then moving up just below her bra. Manoja closed her eyes, each bone and ligament in her supremely awake. For once, she wanted to be inside of her own body.

"I think it means birth," Adalita said with conviction, reaching for Manoja's hand. "Not, like, giving birth. But being able to be born again."

Her fingers were warm, and they sheltered Manoja's palm. "Like, the first taste of air when you come into the earth," Adalita continued.

Manoja felt the wild beating, the dull throbbing ache, inside herself.

"Yes," she agreed. "Like that."

She returned to that night now, alone in her new apartment, hand on her belly, feeling it rise and fall. She had finally sold the Portland house and moved to an island in Washington state, where she could be close to the water. When Pooja was young and the marriage was alright, the family would come here on some weekends in the summer. She remembered Pooja's wild laughter and the glistening water, how they had all swum in it once, even though Saurabh was not a confident swimmer. Manoja and Saurabh moved surprisingly far into the depths of the ocean, and they didn't sink. She helped guide him along.

The water contained her memories.

Pooja called her, asking her, "What are you going to do there, all alone?" *If this girl would stop babying me*, Manoja thought.

"I don't know yet," she said. "I'll cook. I'll swim. I'll watercolor. What are you doing right now?"

"I'm finishing breakfast, then I'm going to drop Abhi to school." She spoke so fast Manoja could hardly make out each distinct word.

"Where's Noah?"

"I don't know."

"What do you mean you don't know? Can't he help?"

"I don't know where he is. Maybe with Nancy."

"Who's Nancy?" *Drew*? Pooja had devoured these books, sitting at the kitchen table for hours, even when it went dark outside. She loved them until she had a realization—Manoja still remembered the clear look of understanding in her daughter's eyes—that she could never be the blonde sleuthing detective, that perhaps the books weren't about someone like her.

"His coworker. He's at work. I've got to go. Just—please call me if you're lonely, okay, if you need something?" Hearing her daughter's quivering voice, Manoja felt that her words were meant for herself. Though her daughter would refuse her advice, Manoja felt a need to speak to her. She reached out to her daughter over the distance, wanting to hold her.

"It's never too late to leave," she said. "I'm here. You won't do this alone." She could hear Abhi in the background, saying, "Mama, look." His voice annoyed her, but then, as she listened more, it sounded sweet. Perhaps that boy wasn't too bad. Maybe he helped her daughter. Pooja needed him.

She was quiet for a while, like she was taking Manoja's words in. Manoja had told her daughter what no one could tell her, what had been impossible for Manoja to do.

"I have to go," Pooja said.

"Okay. Call me later."

"Okay." She paused for another moment, as if she was about to say something else, but then she hung up.

After the call, Manoja stayed in bed, or, rather, on the mattress on the floor, under her blanket. She slept naked, something she had not done for decades. She slid off the blanket and felt her breasts, holding them in her hands. She remembered how Adalita had touched them that night. She remembered how they'd been with each other all night, the way they were enveloped in each other's bodies, the way she tasted like the ocean and smelled like lemongrass. She remembered that Adalita wanted to eat marshmallows after. Just plain marshmallows. They found them at a gas station and ate them together.

She stayed in bed for a long while, thinking of Adalita's face. She could almost feel her face in front of her own, could feel her face collapsing into hers, their selves evolving over the years, Adalita's eyes narrowing, lines forming around them, her mouth opening and closing, sharing secrets, sharing pain. They slowly faded away from one another after that night. It had not meant the same thing to Adalita. So Manoja vowed to forget. She forgot the feeling of

Adalita's hands on her body, forgot what it felt like to touch her own body.

What she wanted to tell her daughter was that she could leave Noah. She wasn't dependent on him financially like Manoja had been on Saurabh. What she wanted to say was that it's easy to end up in the wrong place, and if you don't walk away, you can stay stuck in that place forever.

The hours passed by and it was late morning. Manoja rose out of "bed" and put on a dress. She looked at her face in the tiny, dusty mirror she had retrieved from one of her boxes. She felt unlikely fondness for her small, blurry self.

She walked to a nearby coffee shop, Seagull Café. Her knees hurt as she walked, but she kept walking. It was hot as hell. The sun was made for young people. The sun was ageist, she concluded.

At the counter, she ordered a matcha latte, something she'd seen her daughter order. When it came out, it tasted rather bitter, like the earth. The taste grew on her after a few more sips.

She hadn't brought anything to do and fiddled with her thumbs. All the chairs in the café were blue for some reason. She sat by a little bookshelf with a driftwood branch at its center. It held a range of medieval books. She noticed a woman across from her who appeared to be drawing an intricate branch. The woman wore green eyeliner, and her fingernails were painted black. Manoja wondered if she was waiting for anyone, a partner, a child. She couldn't tell how old she was, but she could see that the years had marked her but not diminished her of her beauty. The years, Manoja felt now, only made people more beautiful.

Anxiety seized her as if she were a teenager readying to ask someone to a silly school dance. She approached the woman's table, holding her latte, pretending to search for a drink sweetener.

Hesitating around the table, she flicked her eyes to the woman's drawing, then to her own shoes and to her latte. "I love your drawing," she said quickly, partly hoping the woman couldn't hear her.

The woman smiled in response. "Come, sit down," she said, after a while. Manoja did. Was she scrutinizing her, judging her? Could she see how nervous she was? Did she know she was out of place? Sitting in the chair across from the woman, Manoja felt she'd made a mistake. She had learned to keep to herself, and this was the right way. It shielded you from being hurt or, worse, embarrassing yourself.

The woman's eyes shifted, as if she was analyzing Manoja, and Manoja did not want to be analyzed. She did not want to be drawn, to be rendered on the page. The woman smiled more at Manoja, and her smile was soft, her eyes inviting. Squirming in her chair, an uneasiness crept over Manoja. The woman kept drawing, humming to herself. She seemed aware of Manoja and yet unphased by her presence.

Manoja breathed in and out and watched the woman as she drew. At the center of the image, beside the branch, she'd sketched a woman's face.

"I'm going to leave her as an outline," she said, looking at her drawing, then at Manoja. She touched the paper tenderly.

"That way, she could be anyone."

SOFT STILL IN PAIN

YOUNG GIRL AND WOMAN // NATIONAL GALLERY OF ART, WASHINGTON, DC

YOUNG GIRL'S BUST resides in a glass cage, her eyes soft and in terra-cotta and in pain. She never said she was in pain. She cannot speak. She is not alive. Like Philomela, the one in the myth, the one dying in faded, coffee-stained pages, her tongue has been cut off.

A still bust is not a body. It only reminds you of one. Don't ever confuse young girl with someone who is alive. Youth is alive and luxurious and free, but young girl is not.

This is how the myth goes: When Daphne turns into a tree, her voice becomes a memory.

Young girl's cage stands against the window, so close it could almost fall through. The window lets in a view of the bright green shrubs and bushes framing the east side of the gallery. Young girl is made of terra-cotta with plaster and paint, carved in 1868, according to the label on the marble block. The light seeping in from outside makes her eyes seem alive for a moment. I look closer and they are drenched in sorrow.

Stillness seems to have been young girl's eternal state. Terra-cotta and plaster instead of flesh. To think that Rodin's shiny-knuckled hands, white and bony, made her. To think that he could simply craft her. She doesn't have legs. She can't run away. And maybe if she did try to run, she'd just become a tree. Another still thing.

I wonder if she shivered under Rodin's touch. I wonder what she would say if she could speak.

I stand between two glass cages, one holding young girl and the other holding woman, both crafted by Rodin. I wonder if still things can be alive. If they can imagine themselves alive.

Young girl's hair is flat like dying grass. Around her forehead, her hair becomes thicker, juts out like a rock, and I wonder if it hurts her, carrying this weight on her forehead. I keep forgetting she isn't alive.

How can you look at a statue with eyes like hers and believe she is inanimate? She's been trapped in the cage so long. Her eyes ache, language halted within them. How can you walk through this room of Rodin's women, filled with female suffering—here, a woman as a sphinx, hands outstretched like paws, lips full and blossoming with dangerous desire—and not feel something large and disgusting churning in your chest? I want to vomit. How can you walk by these women caught in cages and not want to scream?

Half their bodies cut off, voiceless, eyes filled with sorrow. Could they still be alive?

To be voiceless is to be dead. Perhaps a false equivalency. But perhaps not.

Woman's head in the opposite glass cage tilts to the left, her hair large but not free. Hair loops around her forehead and atop her head like stones tumbling clumsily together. She wears a flower crown, although the flowers look more like rocks. Their weight must be difficult to bear; woman's eyebrows furrow. She looks older than young girl. There are cavities under her eyes. Young girl's bust is just a smooth slab of terra-cotta, but woman's bust has ridges, perhaps indicating voluminous breasts, the mark of growing older. She was carved in 1875, seven years after young girl.

I stare at the flower crown and think of Ophelia drowning. It is the only image I can see when I look at her. I turn to young girl again. She is beautiful, but what is the use of beauty when stuck in a cage? I step out from in between them and stare from the side. They look at each other, and they are each other, separated only by years. I shiver. They grow older but remain imprisoned in cages. Age only cements their dark truth. Neither has the agency to speak, to scream.

Daphne runs and her feet turn to cement, then to bark. Before she turns fully into a tree, a slab of skin slides easily off her leg.

Somewhere, today, a teenager is smoking in a forest and uses the slab of her skin, now the stub of a tree, to rest on.

It is not that when she becomes a tree, Daphne no longer feels pain. Apollo still touches her, and she shrinks away. I don't think she's stopped shivering, even now.

When I step out of the gallery, I want to scream. There is cruelty contained in the room, female suffering on display. I am relieved to have walked out, to be free.

But the next morning, the thought haunts me that I am not free. In the mirror, I wipe the toothpaste from the corners of my mouth. I hunch over the toilet like a piece of paper creased in the middle. I heave and nothing comes out. I cannot stand straight. I open my mouth to scream, and only a throaty whisper falls out.

We are women, we are sphinxes, we growl, we are sexual beings—but this is our only rewarded quality: we give pleasure. Our bodies do not belong to us; we are only faces and busts.

Once, a boy pulled me on top of him, and I asked if he wanted me to take off my shirt. As if his want was all that mattered. A subservience deeply ingrained in me. He nodded, and I took off my sweaty shirt, and he fondled my breasts and kissed them and circled them with his fingers and felt the ridges of my nipples, and his erection was hot and hard against my knee and he did not look at me on the street the next day, and for the first time, I wondered if I was invisible.

Behind closed doors, I existed as a body; on the street, in open air, I did not exist at all. I became lifeless, the contents of my mind irrelevant. Any utility I had resided only in my body, in the parts that could produce pleasure for someone else.

I am hurting inside.

Before exiting the room, I stop at another statue by Rodin, of a man, called *Le Penseur. Le Penseur*'s penis emerges in bronze from between his legs, his head downturned. The sphinx woman could also be *Le Penseur,* I want to say out loud. She could be both—full of desire and full of thought. I wish I could tell Rodin. I don't know whether he would agree, whether he could understand.

Before I can leave, gravity pulls me back to the young girl and woman. Something disturbs me—the greenery outside peeking through their glass cages, teasing at freedom.

I know what the curators of the exhibit want us to see: the evolution of female life, the process of aging, a young woman facing her older self. I know they're supposed to be different, their distinction marked by woman's more voluptuous bust, her more fully grown hair, bodied enough to hold a flower crown. But to me the crown is not beautiful, only sinister. Something sharp is caught in my throat. Ophelia drowns, is drowning, and does anyone see? Underwater, she cannot speak and does not call for help. She's disappeared from the text, the love of Hamlet, girl who spoke in mad riddles. She had nothing to say. Nothing to say.

My voice wavers in classrooms, and most people I meet tell me that I'm quiet, and I think they must be right and that's how I should stay so I keep trying to make myself smaller, make myself disappear. To not be an inconvenience to anyone else. This is what I was taught in a home where my dad's voice was the loudest; there is only so much noise a house can take. Walls always on the verge of crumbling. So I bit my tongue, like my mother. I apologized. I am sorry, I am sorry, I am sorry—*let me be invisible*, I wished again and again when I was younger, burying myself underneath my sheets. I still wish this when my emotions are too loud, too heavy. I try to make them lighter. I rip the sheets clean off my bed. A body without skin is just bones. It weighs less. Takes up less space. More convenient. For others. Only side effect is it is no longer alive.

I pull the sheets off my bed so the bed is naked, stripped clean of its skin, and I cry, bite my tongue to muffle the sound of my sorrow so that my roommate can't hear. I bite it so hard I think I taste a little blood. I keep thinking of the boy, how his eyes evaded mine, how all he had wanted from me was part of me, how so many people believe that the sphinx woman and *Le Penseur* must exist in separate frames.

My mind wanders back to the gallery. I have left the room that haunted me, the room of half-dead women, dead women, sphinx woman, young girl, woman, bust, breast, crown. I have left the gallery, but I keep coming back to young girl and woman. No one looks at their eyes, how sad they are in the glass frame. Don't they seem so alive? Their eyes scream. Their tongues burn.

SPRING FLING

THE MOSH PIT IS REALLY *moshy*. The word that maybe isn't a word swerves around in Rashmi's mind as CupcakKe sings about vaginas. The sounds feel empowering, but she can't really hear the words. People are yelling around her about dildos and Sour Patch Kids. Things that she never pictured together. Her mom is texting her about her ajji's snoring. Ajji, who was recently widowed, is visiting the States, staying for a while at Rashmi's house in a suburb of Seattle, Washington. Rashmi is here, on the East Coast at an elite university, and it's her first spring in college and her first Spring Fling and her first time being really drunk. There are mysterious, rainbow-colored zigzags on the grass, beautiful and eerie. Students spread out everywhere, intertwined and free like butterflies.

She's in the mosh pit, swaying with the mass of bodies, and she feels detached from her own body, like she's outside of it. The previous morning, she was in the bathroom crying, and her friend Sarah knocked on the door, and she told Sarah she was homesick. They went to the noodle place with the really spicy soup noodles, and as she drank the soup, she told her suitemate about home. She told her how her mom would brush her hair when she felt sad, and how the sound of the brush in her thick, tangled hair brought her peace. As she spoke, her friend brushed Rashmi's hair and listened, and she was like a sibling and a mother and a friend, every role bled into one. She told her she didn't know if she was crying about being away from home, or the new president, or all of it, but the phrases the president had said about women and their bodies had lodged themselves in her mind, and sometimes they woke her up in the middle of the night, sharp little pinpricks.

Now, in the morning, she can still taste the sour and spicy soup from the night before, and there's also the burn of the cheap vodka in her throat, and someone in front of her spills more vodka on her shoes and it soaks through to her toes, but everything around her is hazy, and her wet shoes take her back to afternoon swim practices in high school and the smell of chlorine in the locker room.

She's trying to arrange to meet seven different friends at various points on Cross Campus, and she can't keep track of it all, so she talks to the nearest person she vaguely knows, a friend of a friend, someone she saw at a dorm room party a couple weekends ago when everyone was dressed in togas because it was a party for people who were in an intensive humanities program where they were reading Plato and Aristotle. It was the first time she'd read these authors, having gone to a public high school, but most of the people in her classes talked about encountering these works before.

This group is discussing Aristotle and what it would be like to pronounce his name like "Chipotle" in class. Sam, the friend of a friend who is in her philosophy class, talks about how Professor Franke would snort in disapproval. Rashmi nods along, adding in a decorative *That's so true!* but Sam doesn't look her way or seem to recognize that they're in the same class. Sam went to the something school, which he brings up often in conversation, but Rashmi forgets the name. She hadn't heard so many high schools named the Blank School until now. Sam is talking about the decibel of Professor Franke's snort, but when CupcakKe starts singing "CPR," everyone flocks back to the mosh pit, leaving barely any space between one person and the next.

Everyone knows the lyrics, and they're all obscene, and it feels thrilling to yell these words across the elite college campus. Rashmi takes off her shoes and feels the grass on her feet, wet with vodka and other indefinable things, and it sends a shock through her body, and it is as if she is returning to herself.

Rashmi doesn't know the lyrics, but she's lost in the sounds, in the wild heat. She has only recently learned how to sway in a nonchalant way; she was coached by Sarah at a dorm room party. "Keep your hands down below your waist and relax," Sarah had told her.

She does this now, closing her eyes. She sways slowly, then more quickly, taking in the smells of Popeye's chicken and bodies and overpowering perfume. She sways too wildly, going out of the bounds of Sarah's directions, and someone catches her as she falls. She falls back, and this someone presses into her, and she feels something hard and kind of slimy against her hand and underneath her skirt, which he has lifted up, and she turns back and glimpses his flashing eyes and dark hair, and the slimy, hard thing sprouting out of his pants. And then he's gone, disappeared into the crowds of shouting students.

And he's gone, but this moment will stay.

In the following weeks, Rashmi skips many of her classes, eating spicy instant ramen in her bed. She isn't particularly close with her roommate who leaves a mountain of her clothes in the middle of their room. In the past, this bothered her, but now, as the mountain grows and grows, she feels more and more resigned. She begins to think of it as Mount Everest, and one afternoon, when Erika is gone, she attempts to climb it but falls into the soft pile of clothes. She falls with the ball of yarn she's been grasping onto since Spring Fling, a random purchase from the craft store near campus.

She gets back into her bed and focuses on the one task she's been consistently able to do: knit. She never learned to knit, only watched her mother doing it wordlessly many afternoons and evenings, lost in the rhythm of the repetitive motion. Her grandmother, her ajji, knitted too, and she always thinks of the ball of black yarn sitting on her bedside table.

Rashmi attempts to make a scarf, but it becomes an unwieldly thing, twisting into shapes beyond her control. The unnamed thing slithers around her bed, coiling and uncoiling around her wrists. The thing is soft and not slimy; it winds around her and houses her.

Sarah is texting her. Her mother is texting her. Dua Lipa is playing on her phone. Oh, yeah, she's been in a Dua Lipa phase since Spring Fling.

That evening, when her roommate, Erika, comes back into the room, talking to someone on the phone, she looks shocked. The sight is objectively absurd: Rashmi sprawled out on her bed, half eating cold spicy ramen, a noodle fallen onto her stomach. The unidentifiable thing she's made swirling around the bed frame of its own accord.

"Uh, what's going on?" Erika asks, entering the room like it's a crime scene.

"Same old," Rashmi says. "What's up with you?"

Erika furrows her eyebrows at Rashmi and walks around hesitantly. Dua Lipa's "New Rules" is playing. Erika walks over to Rashmi's phone and pauses it. She sits on her bed and looks at Rashmi.

"Are you, like, okay?"

They haven't really talked to each other since the first few weeks of school. They had had a few soul-searching, late-night conversations back then. But after that, their interactions had been limited to nodding at one another in the common room as Erika juuled and Rashmi walked over a tower of backpacks and more strewn-around clothes.

"Totally. I had a nutritious dinner." She takes the noodle off her stomach and slurps it up.

"Have you left the room in the last . . . two weeks?" Erika apologizes for sleeping over at her boyfriend's, for not checking in.

"Not really, but I'm doing important stuff. Like analyzing Dua Lipa's lyrics. Most people think her lyrics are reflective of the woes of modern dating. Yeah, sure. But in my view, her true strength comes from repetition and emphasis. We must pay attention to her linguistic choices. Her repetition of certain phrases packs a punch."

Erika continues staring at her with wide eyes. She mumbles something about Marty, another one of their suitemates. She looks down at her phone, sniffles, and shuffles away.

She continues to sleep over at her boyfriend's, and Rashmi doesn't see her the next week. From time to time, she sees her peeking in as she's immersed in her knitting project. There's a voice emerging inside of Rashmi. As she knits more around the room, the voice grows, monstrous and beautiful.

The voice directs her, tells her where to move the needle and the thread. She is making something, even if no one knows what it is. Even if no one can see. Her suitemates stand outside the door, checking on her. She has become a spectacle. It doesn't bother her. Sarah comes to check in on her too.

"Hey, you need to go to class," she says. "Let's walk together to mental health and counseling."

Rashmi knits sleeves around her pillow that hold it in place. She knits patterns over her sheets, shapes of mango and paisley. Patterns she saw as henna on her grandmother's hands. She knits over the windows, making her own rainbows. She knits over the door, and she knows her grades are slipping. She sees her parents' disappointed faces. She feels her body rising out of herself.

Sarah keeps visiting her, enabling her spicy ramen habit.

"I don't really know what happened to you or how I can help," Sarah confesses after weeks of this.

"Nothing's happened. I've just found a new direction." Even while talking to her friend, she doesn't turn away from her yarn. The voice, which distinctly is her ajji's, low and commanding, tells her to revisit the patterns on the bed. She gets on her knees on her bed, butt facing her friend.

"Dude, I'm talking to your butt. Can you turn around when we talk?"

"I just realized that all the time I've been putting into writing stupid essays about Emily Dickinson, I could've put into knitting a room for myself," Rashmi says.

"We're in your room now. What're you talking about? Do you want to go to the buttery? We can get mozzarella sticks. You like those."

"I'm not really into eating things that aren't spicy ramen these days. But I feel very fortified, don't worry."

"Um, has anyone contacted you about your classes? How're you doing in them?" Sarah climbs onto the bed with Rashmi and touches the thread Rashmi has twisted around her hand. Rashmi flinches and pushes Sarah away.

"Sorry, I just have a process. I'm not letting anyone touch my walls."

"Your walls?"

"And about school, it seems I've been getting some emails. My phone keeps dinging. I figure if I ignore the dinging, it'll eventually stop."

"I don't think that's how that works," Sarah says. Sarah doesn't try to touch the thread again, but she tries to reach her. She keeps asking about what happened in a voice that is supposed to feel soothing but feels condescending. Has this always been her friend's voice? And her face, lips pursed, nose scrunched in this particular way? Has her face always been so annoying?

She puts her hand on Rashmi's back, and Rashmi squirms away. *What happened?* she asks, again and again. She touches her leg, and Rashmi circles the thread around her knee, pushing Sarah's fingers away.

What is it, friend? she asks her, eyebrows furrowing, unfurrowing.

Rashmi says his name, the boy behind her in the mosh pit at Spring Fling. She tells her how he pulled himself out of his pants, how he was wet and wormed around on her back. Sarah says his name, surprised. *Him? He's so shy and nerdy, though. I wouldn't think he'd do something like that.*

Rashmi thinks back to the event. He stood so close to her, and when she looked back, he was gone, and his face combined with all the other faces. She felt her hips and where he had been, and touching herself underneath her skirt, she felt a blob of wetness, and it was all sticky. But maybe it hadn't been him. Maybe, she thinks, as his face pixelates in her mind, it didn't happen at all. Maybe she was making too much of nothing.

As the days continue and the weeks progress, the voice in her head, her ajji's, tells her to create more patterns everywhere. She starts on Erika's bed, on their dresser, more on the windows. She can barely see out of the window anymore, but through the slits between the yarn, she glimpses blurry people walking to class.

After high school, Rashmi's mother stopped going to class. It wasn't necessary because she was going to be a housewife, a mother. For a year before she got married, she sat inside her room, refusing to come out except to eat. She knitted in this room. Like her own mother had done many decades before that.

One side effect of the knitting—not the reason she's doing it but nice anyway—is that her suitemates have stopped vaping in the common room. They've found other places to vape.

They still come to stare at her every couple of days. It's increasingly more difficult to look in because Rashmi has filled the doorway with patterns of thread like cobwebs. Sarah brings her a plate of food from the dining hall, but Rashmi refuses it, saying Sarah can't enter the room unless she knows the password. She decides that it's supercalifragilisticexpialodocious497. Something no one could ever guess. Sarah sighs and sits outside her room with the plate. Eventually, Rashmi hears her eating it. From the sound, she guesses it's the college's infamous cape shark, seasoned only with salt (and that, too, sparingly, so the shark-y flavor is unmissable). After an hour or so, Sarah leaves.

When Rashmi's mother and grandmother visit that weekend, they barge in without guessing the password.

"I brought your ajji with me. She'll know just what to do," Rashmi's mother says, setting down a large suitcase with a faulty wheel right on top of Erika's bed. To be fair, Erika didn't sleep in it anymore.

Her grandmother retrieves a bag of turmeric powder from the suitcase and, in her movement, lets out a giant fart in Rashmi's direction.

"Um, mom, what the heck?" Rashmi glares at her mother.

"She's old, she doesn't have control," her mother whispers. *Be tolerant*. Rashmi isn't feeling very tolerant. *I'm not excited for old age*, she thinks.

"Why are you both here? Parents' weekend is over and you didn't come for that."

She could ask where her dad was, but she doesn't want to bother.

"You need help. The college contacted us. You're failing all your classes. You're not going to classes. We're going to take you home."

Her ajji begins to untangle the knots of string around her bed, and Rashmi protests, saying that it's because of her that she started knitting in the first place. It was because of her stories, because of wanting to be close to her. Because knitting was how she got through her life.

"Nonsense," Ajji says in Kannada. "I spend my days engaged with the world. Not knitting all the time."

"Engaged with her Kannada soap operas, yes," Rashmi's mother corrects her.

Rashmi's mother pulls out various items of food from the giant suitcase. A samosa, which is somehow hot, and chapatis she made from scratch with potato palia inside. She feeds Rashmi a bite of the samosa, then the chapati, and Rashmi almost has to spit it all out because it's so hot. Her mother pats her back. Feeds her more. And then it's her grandmother, her ajji, feeding her, patting her, and then she forgets herself, and she is a child.

In Rashmi's dorm room, these women in her family make a tiny home. With a mortar and pestle, Ajji makes a paste with sandalwood and water and dots Rashmi's face. Her mother is simultaneously stirring turmeric powder into hot water for tea. When Rashmi's suitemates come to stand in the doorway like they do every couple of days, they are vaping, and they stare silently at the new humans who have suddenly arrived. They don't do anything and just stare, but Ajji takes a mug from the suitcase and fills it with concentrated turmeric tea. She takes the vape out of Erika's mouth and gives her the tea.

"This is better than that," she says and nods knowingly. She proceeds to tell her that her eyes are looking a bit dull and that the tea will reintroduce some vitality into her face.

Erika blinks in place of words. "It's a bit too hot," she tells Ajji, passing it back to her, but Ajji insists that she should just suffer through the heat and drink it, and it will cleanse her, and she'll never need "that object" again. She points to the vape.

Another one of Rashmi's suitemates, Eddie, who is in a throuple with Erika and someone else, stands outside of the door, and Ajji fills another mug with tea. He refuses, saying she is too kind, but no, he just ate, and then she offers unsolicited advice on the color and length of his hair, questioning the red streak in it and if he needs a recommendation for a local barber shop. Understandably, Erika and Eddie find a way to exit the conversation and run away, and Ajji smiles to herself, as if she's provided key assistance to young people in need of her commentary.

Once they've left, Rashmi goes over to the door with her yarn and knits between the door and wall to make the door difficult to open. This conversation between her ajji and her suitemates reminds her why they all need to be locked in this room together.

It's a strange balance between claustrophobia and freedom in the dorm room. Her mother has recently quit her job at the preschool back home, where a coworker was discriminating against her. She describes the comments the coworker made about her body shape, about her accent. She describes the many lunches of cold chapati and palya she ate alone in her classroom. Rashmi looks at her mother and wants to feel love, only pure, unadulterated love, but she feels a wave of disgust, then anger, and she wants to yell at her and ask her why she couldn't be stronger, couldn't be louder. She asks herself the same thing. She thinks about Spring Fling and the wet thing from him on her back, and if she could've yelled or been stronger, if she was to blame.

Her mother lies next to her on her bed. She brings the yarn from her hand to her mother's, looping it around their wrists. So they are linked here. There is nothing else to say. No other way to name this feeling between them but the yarn that connects them.

Ajji isn't having it. She unties the yarn from around their wrists and tells them to get up so she can sing a song for them. It's "Top of the World" by the Carpenters. She sings off-key, but it's still pleasant to listen to. She gets some of the words wrong and intersperses the English with Kannada.

She climbs on top of Erika's bed and begins to sway on it. Ajji's legs peek out from her sari, showing their varicose veins. She moves back and forth aggressively, almost like she's humping the air, and, embarrassed at first, Rashmi begins to feel admiration for her ajji.

Ajji invites them both to jump on the bed with her, and they go. They jump and jump and then Rashmi feels something hard underneath the blanket, and she finds that it's a plate from the dining hall with a little cape shark and ketchup on it. It doesn't disgust her but opens her imagination, and she sees the three of them as silvery sharks with sharp spines that can't be penetrated, and no one can mess with them like this. They thrash around in the water.

When night descends, Ajji turns off all the lights and tells them to sit on the floor, cross-legged. She has brought a flashlight and shines it on their faces.

"Tell us a ghost story," Rashmi's mother says. Rashmi says she doesn't know any. With the light shining on them, she has clarified vision of the knitted worlds she's made in this room. It is dark, but the threads glow. They swim, bluish-purple, over Ajji's shoulders, scurrying across Rashmi's mother's stomach.

They know what has happened to her because it happened to them.

She doesn't know exactly what they mean, but she feels what they mean.

It is strange—in the dark, their voices merge into one. The same ghost has resided in them, and it reveals itself now.

The same ghost thrashed around in her grandmother and her mother.

The same ghost trapped them to their rooms, made them find homes in their bodies. The walls of their skin thick and impenetrable. Their lips pursed and mouths closed. Their faces unsmiling and not commented upon because they resided alone in the dark, with their threads. The string that brought them back to themselves.

Someone knocks on the door. It's Sarah, Rashmi thinks, but she isn't sure. "Password?" Ajji asks. She's giggling, like she's giddy, drunk. All they've had is turmeric tea but lots of it.

"Uh." The person stumbles from one word to the next. He will never be able to guess.

"*Tuppa*," Ajji whispers to the two of them, the Kannada word for ghee. This is the password. No one else would ever know.

When she was sick growing up, Rashmi remembers, her mom would put on reruns of *The Wonder Years* and make her rice with tuppa and salt. It was so simple and settled her stomach. She watched the characters on the show and wished her hair glowed gold like the main character's mother. She wished she could grow up and look like that, golden skin and golden hair.

She no longer wishes this, but she wishes to belong to herself. To belong to her brown, dappled skin, her long, expansive hair.

What did it mean to be entered? To be wanted, like an animal?

To be wanted did not mean to want back.

For your body to be wanted didn't mean that you were wanted.

To be entered did not mean to be known.

As she looks from her ajji's to her mother's eyes, she knows that they see the threads swirling around. She knows they see the gold yarn she's wrapped around her thighs, from her pillow to the foot of her bed. She knows they've done the same, in the dark of their bedrooms in India. They are separated by years but, sitting in a triangular shape on the floor of her dorm room, they are singular, the same.

Ajji tells another story, stretching her feet out in front of her. They smell bad. Rashmi plugs her nostrils.

"You must respect your elders," Ajji tells her.

"By enduring the smell of their feet?"

"For one," she says.

She tells the story of her midnight, when she turned older, when she got married. As a little girl in India, Ajji always loved fairy tales. She loved the notion of transformation, the frog turning to the prince, the maid into the princess. She transformed, at midnight, from a girl into a wife. A transformation that happened too soon because she was still a girl. She wore the clothing of a wife, and no one could tell the difference.

You see, she says, there came a time when her husband could tell the difference. Rashmi doesn't want to hear any longer. She starts to tell them things that happened in the bedroom. Rashmi rolls over the yarn like an animal. She wants to swim in the yarn, for it to become a safe place for landing.

She tells them she was twenty-two when she discovered she had a condition doctors would now call endometriosis. She couldn't get it diagnosed then. She felt the pricks of pain when he would try to be inside of her, and all of that stopped and he resented her, and this was when she stayed inside her room for a year, only coming out to eat rice and sambar and to sweep around the house. This is when she unspooled yarn all around the room and made it her haven. She protected the space of her bed, where only she slept, because he chose to sleep elsewhere. She covered her pillow and the sheets with yarn, circled the doorknob with yarn, went to sleep with yarn. She felt the yarn on her skin; it became her skin. It became her.

"So how did you leave the room?" Rashmi's mother asks. She's lying on her back on the hardwood floor like it doesn't hurt her. She says it feels magnificent and smiles, so Rashmi believes her. Rashmi has never seen her mother so childlike, so strangely free.

Ajji doesn't answer in words. She rises from the floor and pulls her daughter up. She pulls Rashmi off the bed, throws the yarn on the floor, and Rashmi yelps. The ball of yarn is like a child to her, and she makes her hands into fists, but Ajji holds them, and she lets go.

When Ajji walks to the door, she lets out a very loud fart, and Rashmi looks at her mother again. The sound puts them into a kind of trance.

She follows behind Ajji, behind her mother.

Ajji takes the yarn off the doorknob. It falls, glowing yellow, to the floor. She removes the yarn Rashmi has stuck to the door. It makes a peeling sound when it comes off. It hurts Rashmi a little, like it's her skin.

She follows her ajji and mother out the door. They walk in a line through the common room, past Rashmi's suitemates, who are there, juuling and kissing. They look beautiful to Rashmi for the first time, and free.

She doesn't know where Ajji is leading them. Ajji walks through Cross Campus, and her sari is slipping off her shoulders, and one of her boobs pops out and her belly is showing, but she doesn't care. Two students eating chicken nuggets stare at her, open-mouthed, mid-chew.

She walks through the post office on campus, past throngs of students checking for their packages. A student is coughing, and she gives more unsolicited advice, telling them to suck on cloves to stop the cough. She finds one inside her sari and gives it to them. The student doesn't know what to say but takes it.

"Where are we going?" Rashmi asks.

"You'll see," she says.

She remembers. When they arrived, they told her her grades had slipped too far, and they were going to take her home. Perhaps they were going to the airport somehow. They didn't bring the huge suitcase. They didn't bring anything.

They had brought cloves. Her mother coughs, and Ajji reaches into some unseen fold of her sari and gives her one. And then her mother reaches into her coat pocket and gives one to Rashmi.

As they walk in a line, into a coffee shop on Main Street where students are studying with headphones on and faces buried in their books, they tell each other their stories. They speak to each other with their walking. Their feet thunder on the ground in the same rhythm. Through her steps, Rashmi shows her mother what happened at Spring Fling, why she had burrowed into the folds of her skin. Her mother shows her what happened with her neighbor in India a long time ago. She shows her where the moment resides now, in the middle of her right thigh.

In the coffee shop, Ajji asks for a croissant for free because she's an old woman who has traveled to the States just to see her daughter and granddaughter. It somehow works. She chomps on the croissant and asks Rashmi and her mother to take a bite, and they do. Before leaving the coffee shop, Ajji comments on the six-dollar-and-fifty-cent turmeric latte and invites herself behind the counter to make her version.

"Drink this," she tells the barista in Kannada. Rashmi translates. He does, perplexed. Ajji winks at him. Rashmi pulls her hand, and they leave.

Rashmi still doesn't know where her ajji and mother are taking her. Behind the coffee shop is a path leading to the student-run farm. They walk on the curving path and turn left somewhere, to a trail that isn't very well marked. In her sari, Ajji is surprisingly agile, but Rashmi isn't. She trips over a bush, scraping her knee. She touches her blood, dark and red.

Her mother takes a leaf and presses it to Rashmi's knee, instructing her to breathe in through a nostril and let out the air from the other. She continues the process, and her heart settles.

They walk a bit farther, and when they come up to a big oak tree and a wide patch of grass, Ajji asks them to sit down. They sit on an expansive land, only for them now. They sit in a triangular shape, reaching their legs out. The blood on Rashmi's knee has dried to a blotch that resembles a heart.

"Why don't you put your head on the ground?" Ajji says, and Rashmi and her mother do.

And she tells them a story. When she sickened of the dark room she had locked herself in, she walked outside, past her husband sleeping on the cot, snoring wildly, and to a forest. Her endometriosis had worsened, and while she walked, her pelvic pain was there, a dull but constant throbbing. In the forest, she made a nonhuman friend, a squirrel like she had never seen before. It was a rainbow squirrel, red and blue and brown, with the sweetest little almond-shaped eyes. She told the squirrel everything she was feeling, the story of the pain that lived in her body.

And as she told the story of her body, she let her body rest. She stretched out on her back, feeling the dirt underneath her on a quiet patch of earth. She stared up and saw an expanse of sandalwood leaves above her, patterning the sky. She saw her squirrel friend's eyes looking at her, and the leaves were looking at her too, witnessing her. Her voice filled the air. She felt her body on the cold ground. She held handfuls of dirt in her hands and let it fall onto her knees, muddying her dress. She had spent so long locked in a room, seeing those four walls. In the forest, she saw more. She understood that she could walk out and let herself be witnessed by this world.

To let yourself be witnessed by the world, she repeats.

Have you felt this?

For so long, in the room, the thoughts had been circling in Rashmi's mind, and the yarn wound around her. The thoughts and the yarn became her home. They became her shelter.

In classrooms, back when she was going to class, her voice would waver when she made a comment. She would hesitate, rehearse the words in her mind, and the topic would get away from what she had planned to say. She stayed silent.

At home, back when she was a child, her mom and dad would scream at each other and sometimes at her, and sometimes she screamed back and then all their voices would become the same and she couldn't discern any words. Language would slip away from her. She would long for shelter. She would long to be enclosed in a space that could hold her.

After some time, her ajji said, caressing Rashmi's mother's chin, *you have to step out of the room.*

It becomes suffocating, doesn't it? To breathe only that air. You forget there is this air.

So they breathe and they breathe, and their breaths fall into harmony. Their lives arrange themselves in parallel lines. Her mother reaches out to caress Rashmi's chin. She holds her shoulders and presses her forehead against hers. Rashmi no longer feels the thundering thoughts in her mind. It's just her and her mother and her grandmother, and as they become something else, they become more of themselves. Rashmi turns over and puts her face in the dirt, unafraid of what might be in it.

When she takes her face out of the dirt to look at her mother and grandmother, she sees two rainbow squirrels instead, leaping and making strange little squeaking sounds. Her body feels light, and her skin is squirrel fur, red and blue and brown. She shivers into her new skin. She leaps over to her mother and grandmother, who together climb a tree, clawing at the bark.

They are getting used to their light bodies, their claws, their strong hind legs. Rashmi follows them, placing her claws on the bark, beginning to ascend. But then she hears a shriek from her grandmother, accompanied by a small but audible sound coming from underneath her tail, and the scent reveals that it's a fart, confirming that this is indeed her grandmother, not some other imposter squirrel.

Even in squirrel form, her grandmother has digestive issues. Of course.

The little sound startles her mother, and she loses balance, falling down onto Rashmi, and her ajji loses balance too, hearing all the commotion, and they all collapse onto the ground atop one another.

Ouch, Rashmi screams out, not in words but just in sounds, and then they shriek at one another, and her grandmother lets out a bark sound, and her mother screams and snorts and flashes her incisors at them, and Rashmi does the same, and they all scream at each other, shrieking wildly, until they forget their anger. Until they remember it isn't directed at one another. Until their sounds morph into something else. It is something wild and loud and free. It is something fearful and angry and full of peace. It is something that belongs to them, that is theirs to touch.

HAIR BRIGHT AS THE MOON

EVERY WEDNESDAY AT FOUR, my dead grandfather went to get a haircut at Denny's. Yes, the diner, Denny's. These days, one of its new innovations to distinguish itself from other family-dining restaurant chains was a hairdresser inside the restaurant. The idea was that you could cross off another item from your to-do list just like that. You could eat some greasy comfort food and *also* try out those bangs you were always too afraid to get. It was a deal too good to be true.

Seeing my dead grandfather again was too good to be true. I hadn't told my parents yet; they thought I was just going over to my friend Brigid's house. I'd been going over to Denny's to watch him for seven months now. I knew they wouldn't understand how I could see him again after he'd been gone from our lives for four years. They would say I was hallucinating.

I would walk into Denny's and approach the salon to get a clearer look at my grandfather. He sat unmoving in his chair, stoically awaiting the hairdresser's actions. His request was always the same: "I want hair as bright as the moon." The hairdresser would spray his hair with silver polish, then paint it over in layers of white and blue, and when it was all over, his hair would glow.

This Wednesday, after making the forty-minute walk alongside a stretch of highway to Denny's, I sat in my normal booth. At this booth, I could glimpse into the hair salon inconspicuously. The salon was encased in glass, so the happenings inside it were visible. I sat at the booth, ordered cinnamon pancakes, and lathered fake butter on them when they arrived, and thought about how my dead grandfather had ended up in Columbia, Missouri. He had lived his whole life in Bangalore, India, and only traveled to the States to visit my father or my uncle.

He never liked the rush of traffic on the highways here, or what he called the "plastic establishments" that lined the streets, the chain restaurants, the tall bank buildings, the iHeartRadio tower. At the end of his life, my grandfather bemoaned how Bangalore was turning into the Western world, similar plastic establishments littered all over the city, the traffic becoming unbearable, the density of the city and its emphasis on technological innovations wiping out the residue of the past.

"They want to wipe me out too," he said one evening in his kitchen in Bangalore. He was drinking a mango lassi. It was his evening drink. It settled his stomach, he said. This was the last time I had visited India with my parents, five years ago, and I was eleven years old. I went out to the guava tree in the backyard and stood there, marveling at the bright green fruits at the top of the tree. "I want to climb to the top," I said to my grandfather as he came outside. He held out his lassi for me, asked me if I wanted any.

"No, thank you," I said. I kept staring at the roof, wanting to transport myself there. The red roof gleamed. My grandfather told me a story about the guava tree. He had been scared to climb it too, he said, as a young boy. But it was where he learned how to shut out the world. After his brother died, his mother had retreated into herself. Or, rather, outside of herself. She became convinced that she had become separate from her own body.

She would hold her stomach and pace around the house. She held her stomach as though my grandfather's brother was inside of it, still an unborn child. At gatherings, people would offer his mother a drink of sweet wine and she'd refuse it, saying it would harm the baby. One afternoon, sitting on the cot in the living room, my grandfather heard a thudding sound coming from his mother and father's room, then his father's low and hard voice: "Shut up. Don't make noise." It sounded like his father was slapping his mother across her skin. Then his mother began to moan and the sound stopped, and she moaned again, and then there was a sound like a release, the both of them sighing in unison.

"Now it's out of you. It's gone. He isn't there anymore," my grandfather heard his father say. "You aren't carrying Rohan anymore." At the sound of his brother's name, my grandfather held his head in his hands. His brother's name sent a jolt through him, a rush of awakening.

He felt somehow that he had fractured his family, that he had been responsible for his brother's death, for not protecting his mother from the grunts and screams of his father. Spinning in circles in the kitchen, he felt his mind go blurry, a constellation of pixelated dots. He looked out the window and saw the pleasant green of the guava tree and went to it. The cold air felt like it was encasing him in glass ice. In his friend groups, he was always the nervous, shy one, but this day, my grandfather climbed the guava tree. His cold bare feet slipped on the smooth bark again and again, but he kept moving. He fell down and then strained his legs further, tightened his grip, and rose higher.

He rested his feet on the roof and saw that the red paint gleamed from here too. He sat, his feet dangling from the edge of the roof, and watched the soft swaying of his legs until he felt they were going to detach from his body. Apart from him, he thought, they could fly away and become someone else's. He looked down at his body, and it expanded into shards of blurry glass. He thought of his mother in the living room. Cleaning had become an obsession of hers. She dusted the walls again and again until they became smooth, spotless stone. She would dust and dust and whisper to herself, whisper herself riddles that seemed to lull her into a kind of waking sleep.

"At some point, the body becomes a memory," she said once and repeated it. "At some point, the body becomes a memory." My grandfather stood watching her, his feet pressed hard into the wooden floor. He felt stuck to the ground and imagined his mother's sari flying away, then her body going with it. When he imagined this, he understood why, without being able to articulate it, the loss of a body could mean freedom.

On the roof that day, he whispered his mother's words, and they became true. His body floated away—first his legs, then his torso, and then his lips and nose and arms. It was only here, on the roof above the guava tree, that he could float away like this, become separate and free. He stayed up on the roof and listened to the rumblings from below, hushed yells from his father, pleading noises from his mother. All of it melded into a jumble in his mind, then the yelling and moaning transformed into something like a piano scale, something ordered and predictable, until all went quiet.

Apart. He thought of the word "apart" up there, for he felt wonderfully apart from his parents and their sounds and the sounds of the world. He felt apart, like the green body of a guava falling to the ground. Thud, thud, thud. The meat falling from the bone. All of it falling easily away.

The floating ended when he opened his eyes. The dark had arrived, and the world felt like a crumpled napkin, folded in and trying to exist as new. He saw the moon, slivered and silver. It glowed brighter than the red of the roof, brighter than the composite of all the stars. He held the image of the moon just like that in his head all that night and into the next day. He held the image of its shining and remembered that he had felt its glow when he was without a body and free.

My grandfather told me this story eight months before he died. That trip to India was the last time I saw him in the flesh. After that, there had only been video calls, the Wi-Fi cutting in and out, turning him to a blur, to a faceless voice. And I often couldn't understand what he was trying to say to me on the calls. In the months before he died, his English crumbled away, and he reverted to speaking mostly in Kannada, even to me. My Kannada could not meet his, and we fell to silence on the phone, and the glass between our worlds stood firmly.

The cinnamon pancakes at Denny's were soggy today. I still ate all four of them. I put more fake butter on them so the taste would overpower the sogginess. I asked for more sugar packets for my coffee and stirred them all in. I mostly liked to watch the powder dissolve as I stirred.

My grandfather emerged from the salon. His hair glowed, but his eyes looked tired and old. His skin looked scaly, and patches of silver stuck to his cheeks. It was as though the hair treatment had worked in a lopsided way, that some of the glow spilled out from his hair onto his face.

He walked slowly to the booth across from me and sat, peering down at the menu. I wondered why he had to look at the menu at all. He had been here so many times. The waiter came over and my grandfather ordered something, but I couldn't understand what he said. I rose onto my knees and tried to hear better. It sounded like he was speaking in Kannada, and I realized that the waiter was speaking Kannada too. He was South Indian. I looked around and all the customers were Indian as well. Everyone who entered the Denny's was wearing a sari or a kurta. They were not only Indian, but we were in India. I could not speak. I opened my mouth to speak and no words fell out. It was not my grandfather who had been in the wrong place all these months, who had been displaced. It was me.

I shrank my body by squeezing my hands into fists and squeezing harder and harder. I didn't know how I knew this would work, but it did. I shrank until my head nearly touched the table. Everyone passed by me and didn't look, didn't turn their heads, so I thought I must have become invisible. But my grandfather could still see me. I stared ahead, and he was staring at me, unblinking, eyes like silver jewels.

I wanted to tell him so much. I wanted to tell him I remembered the story, that I'd been coming here every Wednesday, that I hoped he was living okay, getting all the rest he needed. I wanted to tell him that I hoped his body had mended.

When he finished his food—hash browns and akki roti—he rose and wordlessly delivered to my table the journal he'd been writing in. He left without speaking to me, but I knew that even if he had, I would not have understood.

Since my face was so close to the table at my new height, the words in the journal appeared much larger to me. I could see every curve, every crease, in the page, thought I could see, too, the places where the paper had touched my grandfather's skin. The words were in a mix of Kannada and English, but somehow, I could decipher them.

He had written three short poems on the page, and I read them in my head, hearing the words in his quiet, considered voice. I knew over which words he'd stumble, how the stumbles would change his intonations, the rhythm of his speech.

While I read, I felt separate from the world, smaller than it, and I could hear nothing but my grandfather's voice.

> when i speak my mother's broken alphabet
> tumbles out, and the words she kept uttering
> into her pillow while the world was asleep
>
> let me keep singing
> let the melodies keep me free
>
> —
>
> in primary school the teacher beat me with a ruler
> he said i was passing naughty notes

but i was writing to myself
only rehearsing my future apologies

—

atop the tree in twilight
i was a little boy alone
until i saw a glow
from the tree across me

another bright body
another meandering mind

LOVE LETTERS

WHEN HER MOM CALLED her back, Anushka was on the toilet. Now, after days of not answering her questions, her mother wanted to talk when Anushka was peeing like an elephant. Of course.

She wanted answers from her mom. Her dad had visited her a few weeks ago to see her photos, which were featured in a town-wide art showcase. He was in Boston for work, and he drove over to the small college town to see her and to tell her everything she had missed, which was a lot. Her parents were now separated, and her mother was renting her own apartment in Portland. Anushka didn't speak with her dad often, but her mother—how could she have not told her? They called almost every day. She called her mom when walking to CVS, in the grocery store, when she was reading and got bored, when she was brushing her teeth. Her mom had told her about her second cousin's brand of highly effective nose tweezers but not this? She didn't respond to her mother's phone call. *She* would have to wait now.

Exiting the bathroom, she saw her roommate, Dahlia, heating up frozen dumplings on a pan. They had returned to their apartment for a quick bathroom break, but it was now turning into a snack break. They'd come back from the Bollywood Theater where Dahlia worked, a recently opened Indian restaurant-theater that showed classic Bollywood movies. They watched *Mujhse Dosti Karoge!* which Anushka had seen a couple times before. She remembered one time at home, her head on her mother's lap, her mother rubbing her head. She remembered thinking how strange it was that, in the movie, a character requested another character to be her friend, as if friendship were such a simple transaction.

She wanted to tell her mom she'd just seen a movie they used to watch together and wanted to cry. Had wanted to cry but didn't. She was trying to get away from such displays of intense emotion that were commonplace in her family. These intense emotions often erupted into long voice messages and texts from her mother and her ajji. She wouldn't be surprised if her mom sent her a long, heartfelt note later, explaining everything. She sometimes didn't know what to do in response and once simply thumbs-upped a message like this, which led to a rather tense phone call full of misunderstandings.

She didn't want to call her mom back yet. She was too angry, and she'd learned it wasn't good to call someone when you were really angry. She would eat the dumplings first. They were still a little frozen in the middle, but Anushka doused them in soy sauce and they were pretty good. She and Dahlia had had a few cocktails after the movie. Most things tasted good at this point.

They went to another party after eating the dumplings, at Dahlia's friend Tariq's place. He worked with Dahlia at the theater and had graduated a year ago from Williams. He had long black hair that Anushka found beautiful as it cascaded over his shoulders, creating a deep contrast with his white shirt. Though it was his gathering, he stood away from the people, silently eating a cube of cheese in the corner. A single cube of cheese, not on a plate or anything.

Anushka stood next to him, eating a piece of cheddar cheese. She chewed audibly, and he looked at her. She wanted to parallel him. His hand grazed against her overalls dress, and he apologized for the accident. They spoke like this, in silent exchanges, until the silence wrapped around her and she grabbed another cube of cheese, then some wine. She felt her body relaxing. She continued to watch him. He was talking to someone in a black maxi skirt who was reaching into what looked like a bag of edibles. Anushka felt mildly jealous of the girl, of Tariq's focus on her. It had been a while since Anushka felt drawn to someone like this.

She texted her mom. "Sorry, was in the bathroom. Want to talk now?" She knew she wouldn't get a response; it was too late, and her mother would be in bed. She imagined her mom going to sleep alone in an isolated apartment, having prepared dinner for herself—a hummus sandwich with harissa and mushrooms, she imagined. She spilled red wine on her dress, and her imagining was interrupted. Tariq saw, and she tried to wipe it away with her hand. As if this would work.

In the bathroom, she made a towel wet and rubbed at the red spot, and as it faded but didn't disappear, she decided she kind of liked it. It gave character to the denim dress, like blush or eyeliner. *Why doesn't my dress deserve some makeup too?* she thought, and laughed. She wondered how drunk she was because this thought made her laugh. She texted her mom: "I watched *Mujhse Dosti Karoge!* tonight. It's kind of messed up that they would ruin their friendship over this guy, even if he's Hrithik Roshan."

Mahima didn't respond to her daughter. But it wasn't because she was asleep. It was because she was waiting for a text from Evan S, the man she'd been messaging on Cuddlr, an app devoted strictly to cuddling she'd found on a Buzzfeed list of "5 Dating and Intimacy Apps for Middle-Aged Separated Women." A very specific article title. They were supposed to meet at a local bar, the Bottle Shop, at 7:00 p.m. Though she'd messaged a few others on the app, he was the first person she was going to meet in person.

This was Mahima's fourth month living in the Sellwood neighborhood apartment. Before this, she'd been housesitting for family friends while they were in India. After that, she lived in a bedroom attached to a couple's house, and though it was affordable, she couldn't live like that anymore. In total, she'd spent six months away from home, and she'd begun to tire of it, but she didn't yet know if she wanted to return. Returning would mean resuming what had been.

She spotted Evan S in the jean jacket he said he would wear. On the back was a colorful embroidered map of India. Evan S told her he was half-Indian; his dad grew up in Delhi. It was perhaps for this reason, subconsciously, that she'd chosen to meet up with him and none of the others.

He smiled at her kindly as she sat across from him. She ordered a ginger ale and watched his mouth move as he talked.

It moved wildly, like he meant to say different words than those that came out.

He was six years younger than her, but with his beanie on, even in the heat of summer, and the "Om" tattoo on his hand, he seemed much younger than that. He spoke about yoga and sun salutations in a way that divorced the activity from any semblance of culture and made Mahima wonder if, despite his being half-Indian, he was a middle-aged suburban white woman inside.

Still, Evan S had kind eyes. Mahima couldn't describe exactly what this meant, but she knew he had them, and this was why she let him come to her apartment and press his clothed body against hers. She and Mahesh had agreed that, in this time, they could each be with other people, though she hadn't thought she'd actually want to be. They'd barely been with each other in the last twenty years. She wanted touch, the warmth of another body.

Evan S asked if she wanted to watch a movie, but Mahima hadn't installed a TV in the apartment so she said, *Sure, if you want to watch it on my laptop*. The couch became crammed, to say the least, but Mahima didn't want to invite him into the intimacy of her bedroom, even if her bed was just a mattress with a thin sheet atop it.

Mahima found *Mujhse Dosti Karoge!* which Evan S claimed to have watched, though he asked many plot-related questions as the movie played. Like, "Why did Tina just leave her email open like that?" And Mahima laughed weakly at most of them, gripping his hand more tightly. He did feel warm and good against her, and he touched her softly, looking at her with his kind eyes and telling her she was beautiful. He didn't kiss her but touched her, just enough that she felt a quiet lightning dance along her spine.

She thought of Mahesh alone at home, in front of the TV, making his coffee in the coffee maker, sweeping the floors with the

Swiffer, the methodical processes she'd been used to for years. They called every week, and she checked in on him to make sure he was okay, but she limited herself to calling once a week because she was trying to learn what it was like to take care of herself and, somehow, he seemed to understand this. If she texted him too much, he'd let her know that it was all okay, that she should enjoy Sellwood, to tell him if she needed anything, had enough for rent. She didn't take any money from him, but still, she felt selfish for spending her money on living separately rather than on Anushka's education. She imagined that soon this feeling of guilt would take over, pushing her to a decision.

For now, when she moved into this spiral of thoughts, she inched closer to Evan S. He wrapped his "Om"-tattooed arm around her and kept asking annoying questions, but the closeness felt nice. It was closeness she longed for. It was closeness that she'd searched for with Mahesh, that she had only in flickering moments with him.

"She's so brave," Evan S said. His breath smelled of green tea. *Green tea's good for the gut microbiome*, he said. "Putting her feelings out there like that."

"Well, she is hiding behind the mask of her friend."

He shifted and ended up elbowing her. "I mean, have you ever done anything like that?"

"Not like that, no . . . But I've written love letters."

"To whom?"

"My husband. Or . . . well, we're separated now. I told you." Evan S seemed fine with their situation of separation. He hearted her messages about the topic. "But way back. Before I can remember."

The movie roared on. It was one of the final scenes. "Have you?" she asked.

"No," he said so promptly, and almost curtly, that Mahima knew he was lying. She didn't pry. She knew she would never see him again, so she pushed herself closer to him and kept his arm around her, in place.

Anushka was telling Dahlia about the master's program in marketing she would be entering in a few months. It would be practical for marketing jobs, she said, and yes, she was going to have to take on loans, but it would help her figure out what she wanted to do with her life. She was partly trying to convince herself of the truth of her words by speaking them out loud to another person.

"You'll be great," Dahlia said, and the way they said it made Anushka think they meant it. Dahlia had this quality of speaking deliberately and with feeling. Though they and Anushka hadn't been close for long, they were someone in this segment of life who Anushka would miss.

Tariq was eating more cheese, alone again. This party had infinite varieties of cheese. She had a certain feeling at almost every party. What was it? Social anxiety, sure. But it was also something inherited—at parties, she felt like she was her mom, and her dad, standing at the edge of a crowd. In her vision, they were young and old at the same time, her mom's hair the way she'd seen it in pictures, wavy with bangs, her dad's posture weakened by years of sitting over his laptop.

"You don't have to let your parents' stories define you," Tamara, the counselor Anushka had been seeing at Williams, said. But how could they not? How could the stories they'd told her of struggle and sacrifice not settle somewhere in her chest like a precious child she could never let go of?

"You can try writing them a letter, then tearing it up," Tamara said. Her black hair framed her face like parentheses.

"Yeah, maybe."

Anushka hadn't tried that yet. The words were still forming, caught somewhere in her throat.

Later that night, Evan S texted Mahima that he'd love to see her—and cuddle with her—again. Mahima didn't respond. She might tomorrow. She just didn't want to do that thing—what was it called? Ghost-making? Anushka had called it something like that. This was her first experience with any app, and it all mildly terrified her. When Evan S was over, she felt like she was operating from some other place. Like she was merely a hungry animal seeking warmth. Like there was a ghost inside of her, controlling the machinery of her longing.

She heard the sounds from next door. The couple there had very loud sex, but this had only started recently. The woman moaned extremely loudly, almost theatrically.

But soon the sounds of pleasure stopped and they started fighting. Mahima listened to the slamming of doors, the shattering of plates. The woman screamed, "You need to get help. You hate yourself and you're taking it out on me."

She had said something similar to Mahesh once, or many times; she couldn't remember. She typed to Evan S: "I can't right now. Complicated with my husband. It was nice to hang out. Sorry for being another ghost." Shortly after, he unmatched her. It surprised Mahima how it stung a little.

He'd been so impressed by the emails the characters in the movie sent to each other, their readiness to express affection. How had Mahima and Mahesh written to each other? Had it been so easy once? The love letters didn't last long—maybe a couple of months—and happened when they barely knew each other. She thought of it now like a shared hope they both had. "I love you," he wrote to her in Kannada. She didn't say those words back, but she described all the things she loved about him: the hesitant way he walked, placing one foot slowly in front of the other, the stutter in his speech, the thunder of his laughter.

Perhaps it was that she didn't return the words, or the reality of them being together, day after day, but soon, he stopped writing her letters.

Until Evan S asked her if she'd ever written love letters, she barely remembered she had. The stream of ink on paper, the naked confessions of the words, came back to her like a discovery. It was something she wanted to ask Mahesh if he remembered, but asking things like this was difficult. She wanted time to just remember.

Amid the dancing bodies, Anushka remembered too much. She thought of the times she watched *Mujhse Doste Karogi!*—as a child, on the floor, hair in her mother's lap as she rubbed coconut oil into it, as a teenager, in those months at home that were like frozen time after her father had lost his job for the second time.

And before she left for Williams, when her mother had a breakdown and her parents didn't want to talk about mental health.

She stood paralyzed as bodies swayed around her. Dahlia tapped her arm. "Hey, you okay? Come dance with us." They pulled Anushka to their group, where Tariq was, and perhaps because there was a lot of Franzia in them, they moved loosely, and Tariq's hand hit Anushka's belly. He apologized and took her hands, pulling her to dance with him. She did for a moment, until the heat overwhelmed her and she excused herself to the bathroom.

Sitting against the wall, inhaling the lemongrass scent in the room—a surprisingly elegant touch for an apartment shared by recent undergrads—Anushka felt angry at her mother for not responding to her last messages. She texted her again, so her messages lined up like swarming flies on the screen. "I think it's shitty that you didn't tell me you were living somewhere else. And that dad's alone, and he doesn't have anyone." She sent it and felt mad at herself for not going home and caring for him, for holding a grudge against him for years, for deciding now to go to a master's program where she would know no one and be alone, once again.

"For once I'm getting time away for myself and you wouldn't understand," Mahima typed, but she deleted this message. She knew Anushka was hurting. She knew it was the kind of hurt she could ease, at least temporarily, with words.

She started a note on her Notes app. She wrote, backspaced, and rewrote:

We're not trying to anger you. But I know we make you mad a lot. We wish you'd visit home more. I know it's hard to come back. But you still have a home. You always will.

Your dad's been drawing things. Scribbling things. He's been drawing ever since he saw you.

I should've told you earlier that you can walk on your own. (But you should get better walking shoes. Especially when you move—the ones you have are all dusty; I've seen in the pictures.)

Maybe I'll go back home soon and live with him again. I don't know what's going to happen. All I know is that I can be on my own. I don't want you to rush into being with someone. Promise me? Do things that make you happy. Even if they don't last forever.

Your dad and I once wrote love letters to each other. Before you were born. Before I was really me.

Have you worn that dress I sent in the mail?

I'm sorry we've given you our pasts and they're so heavy.

Right now, I'm living on my own. I'm working part-time at the school. I'm making omelets with cottage cheese in the morning. You don't like the feeling of cottage cheese. But it's just the right amount of salty. Joy is good. Even the fleeting kind. Little happy moments. Just for you.

You know the dress I'm talking about? Dark blue with pockets. You look beautiful in blue. I sent you silver bangles too. Wear them and look at yourself.

Have you ever really looked? You're so beautiful, Anushka. Do you know that? Do you really know?

She sent the note.

This was how her mother was. Anushka laughed. She'd predicted this. This was how her ajji was too. Spilling out long messages and voicemails, saying everything they could to her. She was burdening her with more stuff just as she told her to be free.

She stopped thinking for a moment, and she tried following her mom's directions. She looked at herself in the mirror. She concentrated. She wasn't wearing the dark blue dress with pockets or the bangles, but she saw the shape of her face, felt the weight of her hair. She brushed it with her fingers, making it larger, allowing it to take up space.

She exited the bathroom and walked to the dancing people. She moved close to Tariq. He smiled at her. She smiled back. She would never see him again, and she let herself dance.

GRIEF IS NOT OUR ONLY NAME

A MAN AND A WOMAN stand holding hands on a ferry, the woman's hair thrashing around in the wind, the man placing his arm around her, as if to calm her or to steady himself. The man and the woman have lost a child. Sometimes, the woman dreams she is a balloon, expanding with an infinite absence, but there is nowhere to explode.

Last night, she awoke in the middle of the night for first time in a while, feeling wild like a wolf. She tapped her husband's shoulder, first softly and then with an urgency, because she needed him to wake, to stay with her and watch the grayish dark outside.

"Tomorrow, we'll leave," she whispered to him as they sat awake on chairs, looking out. "We'll get out of this place for a little while." She touched his nose and his hand. He gave her a weak smile and asked her, softly, what they were looking for outside. "Should we rest for a few more hours, even if we can't sleep?" he asked.

This was a logical plan but didn't align with the logic of Lorrie's grief, which told her if they kept looking, there was a chance she'd be there, as after ballet practice long ago, waiting for them to come pick her up and take her home.

The last time Lorrie and Gopal had taken this ferry was with Kavita. It had taken her a while to come outside; she wanted to sit and read her book of poetry, the same one she had read for years. *The Complete Poems of Elizabeth Bishop*. She hadn't encountered the poems in class. She found them on her own. At fifteen, the age at which she died, she was most obsessed with "In the Waiting Room." She said the poem captured the feeling of time standing still, and time had seemed to stand still for her, though she knew the world was rushing by, and in the afternoons and evenings, Lorrie and Gopal would come to her room to hold her between them as they did when she was a child. She was fifteen, but she felt like she was living inside a cave, the cave being her room, which she could not leave and which now smelled like old oatmeal and scrambled eggs, everything that was there and stayed crusting there. The doctor had not advised this last trip to Orcas Island, but Kavita had wanted to go, and Lorrie and Gopal wanted to take her. She couldn't hike Mount Constitution, but she spent some time outside, smelling the salty sea, and a lot of time in the art gallery, walking around slowly, staring at the art, concentrating specifically on one painting called *Burst of Joy*.

The painting was blue and green and yellow, and the center of it was a disfigured face, and Kavita kept saying it looked like a butterfly, that the face was a woman's and she was a butterfly. Lorrie and Gopal stood behind their daughter. Kavita was their painting, and they wanted to keep watching her, to keep watch over her, so she would never go away.

There had been a similar painting in Lorrie's childhood home in Wylie, Texas, one her mother had bought after the death of her second husband, a person Lorrie had never been able to call her father. The painting was of a spider's web and, inside of it, a woman's face washed over in hues of red and orange. The painting stood throughout Lorrie's childhood like a constant, there when she tried out for softball and came back dejected because a girl had laughed at her for how she threw the ball, there when her biological father looked plainly at her mother and said that he hadn't wanted to have a kid and Lorrie was standing in the doorway, there when she'd eaten a mango and its juices spilled all over the couch and stained it sticky orange. It was there when Lorrie came back from prom her junior year of high school, lipstick smudged and sparkly blue eyeshadow leaving a trail on her fingers. She came back to the house stumbling, drunk, drunker than she'd ever been, and her mother was on the couch, staring ahead, the painting in front of her, and as Lorrie came closer, she saw that her mother wasn't looking at the painting but somewhere away.

"Careful there," her mom said as Lorrie fell clumsily onto the couch.

"Careful," she repeated.

The vodka made Lorrie's teeth feel like they were sizzling, the lights in the living room sizzling too. She said this out loud, repeated the word "sizzle," and her mother laughed. It wasn't often that Lorrie's mother laughed. She didn't cry much either. Even when she drank alcohol, she remained mostly stoic.

But this night, she let Lorrie rest her heavy head on her lap, and she patted Lorrie with tenderness, was tender even when she said, "Don't drink too much." She was not mad at her. "Even when I was pregnant with the first kid, I was drinking," Lorrie's mother said, almost in a whisper.

"Your first kid?"

"I had an abortion." She said it so plainly and quickly, and it rang in Lorrie's ears.

Lorrie rose from her mother's lap and asked many questions that her mother did not answer.

There was a life, she began to understand, that she did not know of the woman who sat next to her. Secrets she kept close to her in the folds of her skin.

Because Lorrie's mother would not tell her more about the abortion, Lorrie imagined it in the years that followed. She imagined her mother going to some covert location, alone and scared. The mother she knew sat in front of the television, watching conservative politicians talk about the way liberals poisoned people's minds. As Lorrie got older, she shifted farther and farther away from this mother. When the second husband died, Lorrie's mother moved more into her conservative beliefs, but many nights, Lorrie stayed awake, wondering about her confession that night on the couch, how what she had done in private stood in stark contrast to what she believed about the world. That younger version of her mother, the one who had been scared and had walked alone into a clinic, was someone Lorrie wanted to know.

Here, now, the ferry rocked back and forth on the waves, and Lorrie and Gopal held each other, but there was a space between them. There had been a space between them since Kavita died.

"I feel seasick," Lorrie said. "I think I'll go to the bathroom." She wanted to go to the bathroom because she wanted to be alone, and she knew it was one place Gopal wouldn't follow her.

In their house, they spent much time alone. They sat in different rooms; Gopal took his calls, and Lorrie researched Australian Aboriginal languages for work, and in the evenings, they came out briefly, and sometimes they made love, but still, they were enclosed in their dark, lonely caves.

Lorrie sat on the toilet in the enclosed bathroom and felt the ferry rocking back and forth. Before she knew Gopal, she was the odd girl, the girl who had never had a steady boyfriend, the girl who buried her head in books. She'd grown up in a small town in Texas and had wanted to leave it, and when she did, for school, she attached the feeling of education to the feeling of freedom. She fell in love for the first time in graduate school. But he was older, and he did not want to settle down with her, and one night, after drinking beer after beer with one of her friends, she walked home alone and felt, as she walked on the tangled, dark paths, that she was a child again, or a half child, still a person forming, clawing through her mother's warm womb.

She sat on the side of the road and cried, thinking about her mother's belly and how she had felt safe in it, and then how, as she got older, her mother had not made her feel safe, for her mother was a drunk, though she would never say it, and her mother retreated into herself and her prejudices, finding a home in her hatred of the world.

Gopal had made her feel safe. He hadn't kissed her until their third date, and she wasn't sure that they were even dating for a while because he hadn't been eager for touch, though when they did finally touch, it felt right and warm. Lorrie didn't plan to be a mother; in fact, she didn't want to be a mother. When she gave birth to Kavita, Gopal and his family had been there, but Lorrie's mother hadn't. Lorrie's mother met Kavita eventually, but she held her hesitantly, and Lorrie wondered if she loathed her granddaughter for her caramel skin, for how she looked more like Gopal, this man who Lorrie's mother stared at as though he were a foreigner.

Lorrie's mother looked often at Lorrie like she was a stranger. It had begun since she'd gone away to college in California. Lorrie had received a full tuition scholarship and for a while did not understand why her mother resented her. When she went home during her college years—first frequently, then sparingly—her mother stared at her like she was an unknown creature. Once, Lorrie stood in the bathroom, the only one in her mother's apartment, whose door would not fully shut, and she found her mother just outside, peeking in. Lorrie was staring at herself, applying pink eyeshadow. "What is it, Mom?" she asked.

"You wear eyeshadow now," she said. *We are different people now*, she seemed to say.

Years later, when Lorrie stood in the same bathroom again, her mother asked her where she bought her groceries. All these years, Lorrie had traversed far and wide, tasted a variety of foods, and her mother had stayed a cashier at a local Kroger. Lorrie wanted to take her mother with her, for her to accompany her in her life, but they both knew this could not be. They had diverged, and they would continue to move apart.

Years ago, Lorrie and Gopal stood in their first shared space, an apartment in Seattle. They stood in the bathroom, first embracing, then kissing, and Lorrie kissed every part of Gopal's face, the dark spots where his acne had been, his sharp chin, his waxy eyelids. She kissed every part of his face, as if to say wordlessly that he was beautiful, as if to counteract the words his classmates had said to him when he'd traveled to the States for an exchange program in college, calling him "mud face" and "poop boy." She could not take the words away, but she kissed him as though she could.

On the ferry, Lorrie rocked back and forth on the toilet. She hadn't taken off her pants. She did feel seasick. She thought about Gopal, still outside, feeling uncomfortable around so many people. She thought how he'd be making awkward little movements to lessen his discomfort, how he'd smile every now and then at a stranger, offering them a moment of kindness and hoping that the kindness would land back inside of him.

Outside, Gopal shivered and held the bottom of his scarf to warm his hands. He was thinking about Kavita. He was often thinking about Kavita. Before the cancer, when she was ten, they'd taken this ferry to Orcas Island. It was the second time they'd gone. She was reading a magazine in her seat, and Lorrie was in the bathroom. When she came out to the deck to stand with Gopal, she held herself in a dignified way, like a person much older than ten. She stared out at the water, the hungry, turning water, and was silent.

"You know your father used to be a dancer?" Gopal asked. He noticed she was watching someone dancing to a pop song. Gopal didn't know the name of the song.

"Really? No way." Her eyes glinted when she smiled. "You wanted to be a dancer when you grew up?" She said it like it was unfathomable he could have had such bold dreams.

"I did," he said. "But really, I wanted to be a father."

He told her about the conversation he'd had with his childhood friend Arjun when they were fourteen, in an abandoned field with several jackfruit trees. They'd go in the summer to pluck jackfruits and talk about things they couldn't with their parents. Arjun was someone Gopal didn't always talk to, but when they did converse, it was always meaningful.

One afternoon after school, they talked about their families. They leaned against a tree. A jackfruit fell near their heads, and Gopal picked it up, opening it, tasting the sweet yellow flesh. The fruit was overripe, and the sweetness clung to his tongue. Arjun said his father hated him, his mother had gone silent, and he wished he were part of a different family. Gopal said his parents were mostly silent too, but he sometimes talked to his father, and his father had told him that having Gopal to talk to made him feel less alone. "It's why people have kids," Gopal told Arjun. "To feel less alone. To have somebody to talk to."

Then Gopal and Arjun practiced a new Bollywood dance. They twisted and turned, not embarrassed, for in this field, they were unseen and their silliest selves.

"You can imagine me dancing like that?" Kavita shook her head no. "But I got to be your father," Gopal said to her, holding her close. "So everything worked out."

In the bathroom, Lorrie felt queasy. Perhaps it was the motion of the ferry; perhaps it was the nausea of constant memories. She wanted stillness. She wanted stillness and yet knew how it had trapped Kavita in her last year, trapped her to her room, to the scent of cancer, to the incense Lorrie would burn to take the smells away, to take away evidence of the home's spilling sorrow.

Kavita read "In the Waiting Room" again and again in her room, but toward the end of her life, even the words in the poem began to tire her, and Lorrie would find her sleeping in the afternoon, her hand on the open page, and she would close the book and put it on her bookshelf and feel her daughter's sweaty forehead and kiss it and then read the poem to herself, quietly, and wish herself a lifetime of stillness so her daughter could move, could run somewhere, away.

To be away was what Lorrie and Gopal wanted from this trip to Orcas Island. Freedom from the stained home. Lorrie loved Gopal; this was not the question. The question was only about the space they did not acknowledge with words, because what was the point of doing so anymore? Lorrie stood up and washed her hands, though she had not dirtied them, and when she opened the bathroom door, Gopal was standing in front of her.

He reached to her and brought her head to his chest, and then he kissed her. They held each other. They didn't say anything, simply moving their bodies when they needed to make space for someone going to the bathroom. They made space for others and attempted to close the space between themselves.

They hiked Mount Constitution, or half of it, before their legs gave out. They drank a lot of water. They talked about the blue of the sky and how it looked like a painting.

They went to the gallery. They spent time with the paintings, looking at each of them, and especially Kavita's favorite one.

"She loved this painting," Gopal said. "Why did she love it so much?"

"It's called *Burst of Joy*," Lorrie said. "Does it look joyful to you?"

Lorrie watched him thinking, the careful consideration that spread across his face. He thought and overthought things, and in that overthinking was a form of care that belonged especially to him.

"I don't know," he said. "It's all blue. It doesn't seem joyful, but maybe hopeful."

To him, the yellow splashing across the woman's profile was the yellow of jackfruit, of summer and sweetness. To her, the blue was the sound of waves crashing, not here but there, on South Padre Island on the Texas coast. On the coast, she thought as a girl of sounds, the endless sounds of words in languages she had studied—Spanish and French and Portuguese. She thought about different forms of the word "pain" conjugated in each language. And then "pleasure." And she held all the meanings, all the conjugations. All she wanted then, and now, was to understand communication.

Every morning, in their home in Kirkland, Washington, Lorrie and Gopal ached to say something to each other, but they didn't know what it was, so they spoke about routine, about work, about anything but absence. They wanted to say something to each other now, but all of it was pointless and just words, just noise.

Kavita had not been the first name they'd chosen for their daughter. They thought about Keera and Laila and Bindu too, and how each of these unborn children could grow up to be different things—one an actress, one an accountant, another a pediatrician. All of them, before Kavita was born, were real. All of them were possible.

"Maybe she'll have three names," Gopal's parents had joked, eating snacks from the vending machine in the hospital's waiting room. "That way they won't have to choose."

Lorrie turned to Gopal in the gallery. *Maybe we can have many names.* She wanted to say it out loud, but it wouldn't make sense out of context, and she didn't want to explain. He stared at the painting, and she knew they would both keep staring at it for a while, remembering Kavita. She moved closer to him. They would remember her at the mountain, on the living room floor, twirling. They would remember their many names, that grief was not their only one.

STAGE LIGHT

THEIR JOB WAS TO cast light on the performers, to give their bodies and faces an ethereal glow. Fernanda, a junior at Reed College, had been a lighting designer for over thirty undergraduate productions, while Bhavesh, a first-year, was newer to the craft; he relied on her for access to the gossip of the student theater world. Tonight, Fernanda stayed with Bhavesh after rehearsal to teach him about the ellipsoidal, Fresnel, and moving head. After she'd answered all his questions, they got to talking about suspended acting dreams.

"I auditioned for twelve productions my first year," Fernanda said. "None of them called me back. Not even the student-written one about time travel to a future with floating computers and flying saucepans."

Bhavesh laughed. "Ridiculous." He moved the spotlight to the center of the stage; it shone without a body to fall on.

"My mom acted in devotional Kannada plays growing up in Bangalore," he said. "She never said much about herself when she was alive, but when she talked about the roles she played, she seemed brighter. Or lighter." Fernanda noticed the faint circles under Bhavesh's eyes. "One night, she was standing in the kitchen and only one lamp was on, but I could see that her eyes were all red. She started talking about this play she was in once, *Hayavadana*, where she had the lead role of Padmini, the woman who two friends fight over. *Your father didn't know me then*, she said to me, but she was kind of looking past me. *I was beautiful,* she said."

Fernanda looked at Bhavesh, then at the stage, the swirling pool of light, and for a moment, she thought she could see his mother in it, staring out ahead, unblinking, then swaying wildly, a bright dancing fool.

REPAIR SHOP

LONG AGO, my mother tried to teach me how to drive. But her voice reached such a high decibel that I swerved left and right and it did nothing to stop her screaming or the honking of the vehicles behind me.

Long ago, my mother tried to teach me how to put on makeup. But her hand got wobbly as she was applying lipstick on me, and she drew all over my cheeks. She spit on my shoe in frustration.

Long ago, my mother tried to nourish me by feeding me homemade dosa, but the lentils and rice were not cooked thoroughly, and they felt sharp in my mouth. "My mother never taught me right," she muttered in Kannada. The fire alarm went off because she'd turned on the heat so high.

Long ago, my mother tried to talk to me about love and intimacy, but she ended up running to the bathroom instead. She hadn't stopped bleeding for months. "To be a woman is to bleed," she said. "And to learn that men make promises they can't keep." I stood outside the bathroom, listening to her sighs and cries.

When I started bleeding, she was off somewhere with a teacher she worked with at her school. So I had no one to ask for help. I was at my school, waiting for her to come pick me up, which she never did. I sat in a bathroom stall for hours, rolling together sheets of toilet paper, watching this bright red thing drip-drop out of me, this thing that made me ache for her. But I could not tell her this, and she did not find me.

Long ago, my mother was a girl in India, in a swelteringly hot Delhi summer. She looked at herself in her little round mirror, with her little black braids. In her ears swam the sounds of crickets and the streets and the noise of her parents' screaming, a never-ending thunder. Long ago, my mother was a little girl, and she vowed it would be different with her daughter. She cradled the air like there was a baby there. She was soft and gentle with her, caressing her imaginary head, touching the spit bubbles at the corners of her small mouth.

Long ago, before everything else, my mother longed for many things.

Now, I am fifty-six years old. My mother died last week. I went to work the day after she died. My hands shake at the wheel of my Prius now, but it doesn't matter. I still must get where I need to go.

I sit from nine to five at Carrie's Towing, waiting for the surprised faces of the idiots who left their cars in the dispensary lot at unauthorized hours. They either come in with a resigned look on their faces or an angry one, as if the universe has wronged them. For the first few years at this job, I felt a deep satisfaction when they would tap or insert their credit cards and the machine would extract an exorbitant fee from them. Now I don't feel that satisfaction. It's hard to feel anything at all, being somewhere for so many years.

It's hard to feel anything until it's dark out and my shift is over. Until the dark slithers over the building and the parking lot with all the cars people haven't retrieved, and the vehicles swallow the darkness and become something else. Become what they really are.

My mother died at Mercy Health Hospital in Fairfield, Ohio. The city I grew up in with her. The city where I've lived now for many years. I held her hand, but it quickly fell out of mine. Even in these last moments, she couldn't hold my hand firmly. And I couldn't hold on to her.

I moved back to the Midwest after dropping out of a small liberal arts college in the Northeast. I'd gotten this job to pay my bills because it was a job. I've been here for decades and grown old. I look into the mirror in the morning and see my mother's tired face.

I rent a house with ever-changing strangers, people I never get to know because they never stay long enough. This one guy has stayed for a couple years, though, but I still haven't gotten to know him. Every evening, I sit in front of the TV, eating cold pita bread and garlic labneh. Recently, I haven't known what to watch, so I just stare at a black screen.

When I drive home tonight, later than usual, my hands are shaking so much, and I almost swerve off the highway. A car honks at me and honks again. My mom taught me to drive in a Blue Honda

Civic. She crashed it somewhere on the road with her co-teacher-lover.

When I arrive home, I park the car badly, too far away from the curb. I'm too tired to adjust it, so I go inside and plop down on the couch. Anthony, the man who has been here for a while, shuffles around loudly in his room. I hope he doesn't come out to the living room. I don't know what to say to him. I stare at the black TV screen for forty-three minutes, then go to my room and lie down on the bed.

In the morning, the tires of my Prius are slashed, and when I try to drive, the car makes such an unpleasant sound, like a loud, dying lawn mower. Anthony steps out of the house for his morning walk, and he sees me, or hears my car. He offers to drive me to work, and I reluctantly accept his offer. He is nearly seventy and doesn't drive much now, only for necessities. "Helping out a friend is a necessity," he says and smiles. He is kind, and yet I feel irked by him. I question what is beneath his kindness.

The car ride is mostly silent, but he turns on his music, which is a combination of slow country and Julien Baker. "I like her vibes," he says, as if he's trying to be relatable to a Gen Zer. He tells me that his daughter, who is twenty and studying psychology at Kenyon College, likes Maggie Rogers and Clairo. I nod, again not really knowing what to say.

"What kind of stuff do you listen to?" he asks me.

"Indian instrumental music," I say. This is only half true. The other half of the time, I listen to oldies pop on my way to work, which is what used to play on the radio station when I was in the car with my mom. I liked those car rides when they happened, when she worked at a Montessori school next door to mine. They were quiet and some of the only times I remember seeing peace in my mother's eyes.

"Right on," he says. Who is this guy, really? He seems perpetually happy, always nodding in some sort of daze. His gray hairs shine in the summer light, almost beautiful. I thank him and get out of his car when we get to my work. He tells me he'll come to pick me up when I'm done. I don't know what to do, so I thank him again.

What should I tell you about how my life got off its expected course? What can anyone really say or explain? I dropped out of college when my mother needed help, when she could no longer help me. I'd gotten scholarships to cover most of my tuition, but it wasn't enough. I worked at restaurants and coffee shops, and then I got this job here, and I sent money to my mom so she could live, the breath flowing in and out of her lungs, though I think at a certain point, she wasn't really sure if she wanted to do that anymore.

I was a bright star, the salutatorian at my high school, sent off to a fancy, small liberal arts school in the Northeast. I was going to be someone. I was going to be someone, despite my upbringing, despite being raised by a single immigrant mother, despite my father walking out on us, despite it all. I was going to be a success story; I was going to be a model minority, one who had conquered it all. I was going to be—

Suspended, is what I am. Like the cars. In a waiting place.

I get someone from Carrie's Towing to come and take my Prius to the repair shop. The shop is right next door to Carrie's Towing, so I can easily monitor the progress of the repairs. Anthony seems overjoyed to be driving me to and from work for the foreseeable future. I tell him that I will rent a car temporarily, but he insists.

It's a week of Phoebe Bridgers. "Kyoto" comes on, and he starts nodding his head and even clapping his hands together at one point, in celebration of something unknown.

"Hey, um, the wheel—"

He says he's been to Kyoto and loved it there. I don't know what he used to do for work, and I don't ask. He has a way of volunteering information anyway, so I anticipate that I'll learn soon enough.

On Friday, he reminds me that his daughter is coming to visit for the weekend and will be arriving in the evening. I nod and thank him for the ride.

At work, I meet a variety of angry faces protesting the costs of towing their cars from the dispensary lot. I nod at their complaints and say nothing. I haven't been sleeping well the past several nights, and I fall asleep at my desk. No one really talks to one another at Carrie's Towing, and no one wakes me up to tell me to leave when the day is over. When I wake, it is 8:34 p.m., and dark is falling. I wake in a dream state and with the urge to see my mother. I know she isn't here, but I feel that she's next door.

Anthony has been texting me. I tell him I don't need a ride right now, but in another hour, I'll get an Uber. *I have a work-dinner thing,* I lie. *Have fun with your daughter,* I add, to which he immediately replies with a host of uninterpretable emojis: a fire emoji, heart eyes, star, ghost with tongue out, and brain. Who is this guy? I wonder once again. I suppose I haven't shown much interest in finding out.

The repair shop where my Prius is has closed for the day. I still go, and I can see, because the garage door is open, my Prius standing there. I don't know why the door is open. The car gleams, and I find myself drawn magnetically to it. Other cars surround it, but it stands in a space of its own.

It's dark in the garage except for rays of light falling onto and around my Prius. I hear a sound of something scurrying and think that a mouse or a rat has found its way in, but I can't see any around me, but then again, I can't see much except for the gleaming Prius. The scurrying sound transforms into something like a voice, and it is my mother's voice, and it reaches out to me.

I sit on the floor. I don't really care what's on it. The dust too is residue of her. How strange, I think, that my mother has turned into a blue Prius whose catalytic converter has been stolen and whose tires have been slashed. I feel guilty for not taking better care of her.

"You go on and on about how I don't see you," she says, "but what about all the times you didn't see me?"

I suppose my Prius mother has a point. I drive her to work every day, park her in her spot, and then spend my day watching over all the other cars in the towing lot. I pay no attention to her, but maybe she's been calling out to me.

I can't quite figure out where her voice is coming from. I touch the front bumper and then press on it, and I hear her squeal. So this is her mouth.

"Hey, watch it!" she says. "Be careful with my lips. They're one of my best features."

I apologize, and then she begins to offer unsolicited advice. This *is* my mother.

"How long has it been since you've had a hair trim? The ends are getting pretty messy. Have you been applying coconut oil?"

"This is why we spoke so little after I reached puberty. Your knowing little comments."

She's quiet for a while, and I'm worried I've upset her. I'm annoyed that the same dynamics that persisted with us in life still seem to exist, even while she's in car form.

"I was thinking about dyeing the ends pink, actually."

"Don't do that. That is not flattering on an Indian skin tone."

I roll my eyes and don't know if she can see, or where she's seeing out of. "Don't roll your eyes at me," she says.

The thing about her voice is that it isn't the voice she had before she died. It isn't her voice, even, from the last twenty years of her life. It's a younger voice, one I almost don't know. One I've heard only in old videos, on fuzzy film, when I was a child and I gasped to see my mother as a young woman in her early twenties, at the beginning of the rest of her life.

"How old are you?" I ask her, standing up, touching her windows.

"You'll poke my eyeballs out, be careful," she groans. "I'm also known for my dazzling eyes."

This version of my mother is especially conceited.

"To answer your question, I just turned twenty-four this April."

My mother was twenty-five when she had me, so I'm not born yet. I ask her if she knows my father. She doesn't recognize the name. I throw out the names of men who later became her boyfriends, and she doesn't know their names, either. But she knows my name. She knows me, even if I'm not her child. She knows me, as if we're friends. We talk to each other like friends, and I forget briefly that I am me, fifty-six years old, living where I do, with the past I have had.

She tells me about when she was a little girl in India, before she moved to the Midwest with her parents, where her father pursued a PhD in chemical engineering. In India, she would go with her family some weekends on a long train to a temple, where they would pray. On this train, which slid through the hot summer nights, she and her brother made up secret handshakes. Each one more intricate than the last. Precisely choreographed songs accompanied the handshakes. More than once, fellow passengers told them to quiet down. And she remembers their giggles, rising like bubbles in the air. If she had fingers now, she says, she could just about reach out and pop one of the bubbles, and hear her brother's excited, musical voice.

In the garage, where my mother waits to be repaired, we talk to each other as if we're free.

When I get home that night, Ubering, I see a girl with glasses and freckles who resembles Anthony. She sits silently at the kitchen table, eating instant mac and cheese in an ominous way. I don't really know what to say to young girls. Perhaps because I feel like I've never really been one.

"What's up?" I say. She nods in response. That's good enough for my quota of human interaction. I decide to go to sleep.

But as I'm turning to go into my room, Anthony grabs my hand. The action startles me, and I almost jump. I haven't been touched by someone in a long time.

"Hey, do you want to watch some TV with us?"

I don't know why, if it's the boyish smile on his face or the fact that I have just talked to my mother before she was my mother as a car, but I join them. Despite my resistance, I end up sitting on the couch between Anthony and his daughter, and I feel so uncomfortable in my position that I hardly move. To make matters worse, they decide to watch *Sex Education*. A new season is out, and his daughter has been watching the show. So we sit there watching a boy masturbating on screen, and Anthony nods along, trying, I can tell, to model a sex-positive attitude, and his daughter says, sheepishly, "Uh, we can also watch something else."

We end up watching *Bob's Burgers*, and I spend the whole time trying to imagine what kind of gel the father character puts in his hair to make it so rigid looking. When either of them laughs, I laugh too, and I'm reminded of my grandmother when she visited us from India. She would sit in front of the small television, watching a show like *Friends* with laugh tracks, and laugh alongside them, though I knew she didn't understand the jokes. It made me smile to watch her because she was laughing, and because it wasn't often that I heard laughter in that house.

When my mother took off with her coworker, I was just beginning college, and I had just discovered the wonders of touching myself. It was the way I could make myself feel something so powerful with just my own hands. It was the way I could give time to myself, when at every other turn, I had to give time to my classes, to my friends, to my part-time jobs. I could linger in this space of feeling and feel that I was inside of a body, a woman's body, and it belonged to me. So often I felt detached from the house of skin I lived in.

Today, in the garage, I ask my Prius mother about the first time she got her period. It was something I could never ask my mother in life. She tells me it happened thirteen years ago, when she was at the store with her best friend, looking for dresses. She was in a stall, trying one on, and she remembers the queasy feeling in her stomach, the homesickness that rushed over her. She remembers feeling alone, so alone, but then emerging out of the stall and there was her friend with a beaming smile.

My mother—well, really, she was not my mother, she was a car, suspended somewhere, out of time—she was peaceful when she was swimming out in the river where she would go to wash her clothes and bathe, and sometimes, if no one was looking, she'd swim out as far as she could and dive down into the murky water, seeing how long she could stay underwater.

I touch the roof of her. "What's this?" I ask. "Your hair?"

"Yes, and as a person, I had it very well kept. Coconut oil every night before bed."

"Fine, yes, I should put coconut oil in my hair. Any other suggestions?"

"Smile more." The last time I heard this suggestion, I was walking down the street and a man pulled the corners of his mouth, telling me I'd be much prettier if I just smiled. I couldn't smile for two weeks after that, even when I saw something funny on TV.

He'd made me feel squirmy inside.

But the way she says it, her voice light and sweet, I feel embraced.

Anthony's daughter, Irene, who he named after the song "Goodnight, Irene," really likes Cincinnati chili, so we drive fifteen or so minutes to the closest Skyline. I stopped eating meat when my mother died. She never ate meat, and it felt like I could be closer to her in this way. I order plain spaghetti, and the cashier looks at me questioningly.

I watch Irene and Anthony gobble down their chili, and they look nearly identical doing so. Irene tells me she is studying psychology in college, but taking as many creative writing classes as she can. I begin to ask questions, to my own surprise, when she mentions her writing workshops.

"What genre is your favorite?" I ask. "Who are you reading in your fiction workshop?"

In my mind somewhere, there is a shining dot, and inside of it, a memory of me in writing workshops at the liberal arts college in the Northeast I attended and dropped out of.

Inside of the dot, there's me, sitting in class with two braids, staring intently at the professor.

Inside the dot, there's me, scribbling in the poor lighting of my dorm room, poems about whales and longing and everything I don't know.

Inside the dot, there's me, long ago. There is me.

Driving back to the apartment, Anthony seems distracted because Irene is telling him about an effective altruist club she's part of at her college, and he nods along blankly. She even asks him a question about what his major was in college, and he continues to nod, adding a mumbled "Definitely." Perhaps this is a routine occurrence because Irene, though she sighs, doesn't bother him.

I look out my window until the car behind us honks loudly and Irene slaps his shoulder, saying, "Dad, snap out of it, the light's green," and he goes.

Back in the apartment, Anthony excuses himself, and Irene and I sit together on the couch. Unprompted, she begins to speak. "He must've been thinking about my mom," she says. "He always gets that way when he thinks about her. They separated sometime after he got sick."

She says it as if I know that he is sick. I don't know what kind of sickness he has, or how often he gets this way, and I don't ask these questions. I move myself closer to Irene and put my hand on hers.

What does it mean to be a mother in the world?

I've never had children of my own; my body hasn't allowed me to.

I hold Irene's hand. She shifts closer to me, hesitantly, and puts her head on my shoulder. I pat her head because this is what my mother used to do to me. Even if she didn't often know what I needed, she always knew to do this.

The next time I see my mother in the garage is the last time. I ask the people at the repair shop when she'll be ready, and they say tomorrow. She looks shiny tonight, like she's just been given a wash, and somehow, her pristineness makes me want to cry. It wasn't much like her as a person to be so clean. She would leave her hair unwashed for weeks when I knew her. When my dad left us, she didn't shower for nearly two months. The whole house smelled of her.

But I don't want to burden her with stories of who she'd been. Here, she is shiny. This is who she is. Here, she doesn't know about my father, or all the men and the scars, or when she couldn't take the bills and dishes piling up and would lock herself in the pantry and scream. Or when she drove away and left me to grow up long before I was supposed to. I don't want to tell her all these things she doesn't know.

She looks beautiful like this.

"One more story," I ask her. "From whenever you'd like."

She tells me a story about eating Maggi noodles with her brother in Delhi. He threw cold noodles on her head, and she threw them back at him and they landed on his face, then the floor. She took some more and placed them on her head, and they danced around in their socks—"sock-skating," as they called it. "I looked great with noodle hair," she says. "I looked just fabulous." As she speaks, her engine revs up. This sound means she's laughing.

Someone sees me talking to her.

"Who're you talking to, lady?" He works at the shop and has come to get his water bottle. "You shouldn't be in here, you're trespassing."

I flutter away and hurry to the curb, where I call Anthony. The man shakes his head at me and maybe curses something under his breath, but it doesn't matter because I can leave now.

He can think I'm crazy, but I know who I've been talking to. It's enough, even though he pulled me from her. I can say goodbye because this time, the last sound I hear from her is her laughter.

That night, when we get back to the apartment, Anthony and I are both exhausted and alone again. Irene left two days ago, and since then, fatigue has taken over Anthony, and he spends most of his time sleeping. It occurs to me that I don't really know what he does all day. He speaks vaguely about a screenplay he's working on, something about a forlorn galaxy, and it honestly sounds pretty bad, so I zone out when he tells me about it.

There isn't much I know about Anthony, even after all the time we've spent together recently. I know, though, that when I've needed someone to pick me up or drop me off, he's been there.

I know that when, tonight, he goes into his room, I want to follow him and place my body next to his.

He accepts me here and puts his arm over me like a blanket. It feels like a block over my stomach, a bit uncomfortable, but I want it to stay there. As my rumbling stomach settles, I imagine what it would be like to hold human life there. The way my mother had once held me.

I begin to tell him things. I tell him with words, first, about my mother as a car, and my mother in life, her sudoku puzzles at night, her proclivity for running away, and how when she died, it still felt like I couldn't hold on to her. And how I stopped running at all. I stayed here, in this town; I stayed because there was nowhere else I knew to go. Then I speak to him with touch. In the bend of his arm, I display my unborn dreams. To be a mother. A writer. To teach. To learn. To keep learning. To move.

I bury my head in his chest. From my head, I let spill the memories of moving around with my mom in her dusty car, which she named Veena. In one memory, I'm in the passenger's seat, trying to fall asleep on our drive to Kansas City, where she's going to a teachers' conference. She keeps looking down at her phone because some guy she's seeing is calling her repeatedly. I have to stay awake to help navigate. In another, she's teaching me to drive and yelling at me in the junior high school parking lot. I'm going slow, so slow, around the curves of the lot, and she tells me to press on the gas, that I shouldn't be so afraid to go faster. *You have to take control,* she demands, *or they'll take control of you.*

I don't know who "they" is, but whoever the "they" is, they are hurting her, because we sit parked in a space for a while as she cries. I remember the snot that poured down to her lips. I remember looking at her, my beautiful mother, and feeling disgusted.

Veena, Veena, Veena. My mother told Veena so many things.

I couldn't tell my mother many things.

I can feel Anthony's memories rumbling around in his stomach. I sit on top of him and press my face to his.

He kisses my lips, and I pull away. I want to get to the lips last. I kiss his right cheek, then his left, and his chin and his neck, and I feel the things he can't say.

In the morning, Anthony drives me to the repair shop to pick up my Prius.

She's shiny and fresh, and the engine roars on with gusto.

"Still laughing?" I ask my mother, but she doesn't reply.

I understand. My mother's gone. It's just a car again.

She's left me with roots in my mind. With dreams ripening somewhere inside.

I'll enroll at the community college. I'll open the journal someone I had loved gave me long ago. I'll remember how I'd wanted to have a family with this someone long ago.

I'll make my own family. I'll give Anthony a cheesy Hallmark card for his birthday, and he'll think it's sweet.

I'll drive.

I'll go to the beach, unplanned, on a Sunday. I'll be underwhelmed by the views.

I'll try out the lavender latte at the local coffee shop and immediately regret the seven dollars I spend.

I'll hear my mother in the car's engine, her laughter.

I'll massage coconut oil into my hair and then chop it all off. I will feel my mother's disapproval, her face staring at me in the mirror.

I'll see her eyes, scared, in my own. I'll breathe slowly and be less scared. The fear will return in waves.

I'll drive to work. I'll waste away behind a red light. I'll be late.

I'll curse out the motherfucker in front of me who doesn't go, even after the light turns green.

I'll notice they're a student driver. I'll forgive them.

I'll drive all around the town I grew up in, left, and came back to. I'll drive in circles, going nowhere, and eventually somewhere.

I'll get angry at my mother all over again, fresh rage bubbling within me. I'll forgive her.

I'll forgive me.

I'll take us home.

ACKNOWLEDGMENTS AND GRATITUDE

THERE ARE so many people and places who helped make this dream a reality. Thank you to the journals and magazine editors who gave individual stories in this book a home, in order of appearance:

"Hoarder" was originally published in the Spring 2025 issue of the *Massachusetts Review* (66:1). "Kerosene" first appeared online in MQR Mixtape from the *Michigan Quarterly Review* on April 28, 2024. "In Lamplight You Are Made Whole" was first published online in *Apogee* on August 25, 2023. "A Sweater for You" was first published in the February 2022 issue of *Pleiades* (42:2). "Blood and Bone" was published in the Winter 2021 issue of the *Indiana Review* (43:2). "Harshal" was published online on February 8, 2022, by the Asian American Writers' Workshop's the *Margins*.

"A Pure Thing" was originally published online in the *Yalobusha Review* in issue 37 in June 2023. "Let All Our Ghosts Depart" was originally published online in the *Rumpus* on October 23, 2023. "Soft Still in Pain" first appeared in the Enough series in the *Rumpus* on January 21, 2020. "Spring Fling" was published in the Summer 2026 issue of *The Hopkins Review* (19.3). "Hair Bright as the Moon" was published in the February 2023 issue of *Passages North* (no. 44). "Stage Light" first appeared online in the September 2024 issue of *Ghost Parachute* on September 1. "Repair Shop" is the winner of the Barry Hannah Prize and originally appeared online in Issue 41 of the *Yalobusha Review* in May 2025.

Thank you to Marguerite Avery, my editor, who gave these stories a home with West Virginia University Press. Thank you, Margy, for your enthusiasm, dedication, and deep editorial insight. Thank you to the entire West Virginia University Press team, including Than Saffel, Kristen Bettcher, and Natalie Homer, for the care with which you brought this collection to life. Thank you to my copyeditor, Mike Jauchen, book designer, Kelley Gallbreath, and cover designer, Elisha Zepeda, for your incredible vision. Thank you to the Little Birds Literary team of Abby Freeland, Kendra Winchester, and Davis Shoulders for all your work getting the word out.

Thank you to my agent, Tanusri Prasanna, who championed this book long before it could be called a book. Thank you, Tanusri, for believing in the power of stories about women and their interior worlds.

Thank you to the incredible authors who offered words of support, including Susan Choi, my brilliant undergraduate thesis advisor; my former professor Karen Bender, who has been such a source of mentorship and encouragement through the years; and Sejal Shah, Marian Crotty, K-Ming Chang, and Jessie Ren Marshall, all of whom have written things that have helped me hope, feel, and live.

Thank you to my teachers who told me to keep writing and who inspired me to be a teacher: Susan Choi, Caryl Phillips, Margaret Spillane, Karen Bender, Elizabeth Poliner, Jessie van Eerden, Pauline Kaldas, Richard Dillard, Akhil Sharma, Kristen Arnett, Marcy Huss, my high school English teacher who believed in me when I didn't know how to believe in myself, and Wendy Kuba, my elementary school teacher who told me that I had something important to say. Thank you, also, to Katie Hays, who hasn't been my teacher but who has transformed me through her friendship and mentorship. Thank you to my MFA thesis advisor, Scott Blackwood, who is no longer on this Earth but exists in these pages. Thank you, Scott, for every note.

Thank you to the literary communities that helped me envision what it could mean to be a writer, including Write Around Portland, The Steinbeck Fellows Program at San Jose State University, VoiceCatcher journal, the Carolyn Moore Writing Residency, the McCormack Writing Center, the Creative Writing Concentration at Yale, The Kimmel Harding Nelson Center for the Arts, Writing by Writers, the Jackson Center for Creative Writing at Hollins University, the Amherst College Creative Writing Center and English Department, and the Creative Writing Program and Stadler Center at Bucknell University. Thank you to the people within these communities who have supported me in countless ways, including poet Jessica Nirvana Ram who generously connected me with her communities and uplifts so many folks of color in her life.

Thank you to my friends who have read drafts and provided feedback, community, and joy along the way. There are far more people here than I could name, so I won't try, but thank you to my writing group for reading drafts of these stories, and to Jennifer Acker for inviting me into this group; thank you to the SAME Girls group chat and to the friends who have uplifted me, and celebrated with me, who have stayed up late talking on the phone about hungry ghosts and blood-building tea, who have fed me, who have taken long, meandering walks with me, who have moved with me through traumas and delight, who have offered me biscuits and reminded me to move my car at night so I won't be fined, who have been like my grandparents and siblings and parents when I'm far away from my own. To my friends from every place I've lived: as I've moved around, searching for somewhere to land, you've kept me tethered to myself. Thank you for making me feel more at home in this world.

Thank you to my family: Nima, Sham, Priya (my Pretend Game co-creator), Mari, and Pepper, and my ajjis and thathas, Anantha and Vijaya Rao, and Manjula and Ranga Rao. Thank you, Mom, for sitting on the steps with me as a child, with just a dictionary and whimsy, introducing me to so many words. You taught me words in English and in Kannada; you helped me find our language, the one I use to speak to you.

MEGHANA MYSORE'S stories, essays, and poems have appeared in publications including *The Yale Review*, *The Massachusetts Review*, Roxane Gay's *The Audacity*, *Michigan Quarterly Review*, *Yalobusha Review*, and *The Boston Review*. She is the winner of the 2025 Barry Hannah Prize in Fiction. Mysore has been a Steinbeck Fellow, a scholar at both the McCormack Writing Center and Bread Loaf, and received recognition from The Kimmel Harding Nelson Center for the Arts and The de Groot Foundation. She holds an MFA from Hollins University and a BA in English from Yale. Mysore has taught at Amherst College and Bucknell University, and is assistant professor of English and creative writing at Randolph College in central Virginia.